THE
VOLVOX

A novel by Sandra Heilpern

© Sandra Heilpern 2014

Sandra Heilpern asserts the moral right to be identified as the author of 'The Volvox"

Cover design and typeset by Green Avenue Design.

Cover photo by Lili Shapiro

Published by Cilento Publishing.

ISBN: 978-0-9925602-3-2

1. GONE

It is one week since Bella has gone. One week since that Tuesday when she disappeared from my life.

Bella was sixteen years, one month and two days when she set off for school that morning, that day, which neatly slices my life into two distinct parts – the time with Bella and the time since she has gone missing.

That morning did not seem to be any different to any other morning at our place. And I should know. I have lived it over and over in my mind almost every day since. I do replays. I change the script. I write myself in as a superbly vigilant mother, who notices and notes every little nuance, every word, every expression that Bella puts out. I even notice what she is not saying. I look across to the kitchen doorway, the moment she appears. I do eye contact. I look searchingly and concernedly into her face and ask her what she would like for breakfast. "Oh", I answer in surprise, "toast and vegemite," even though it has been toast and vegemite for the past thirteen years. I ask about her needs for the day. Does she need her sports clothes ironed? Would she like a packed lunch?

Who am I kidding? She would have shrugged me off with a "Oh Mum, do you have to?" and slumped down at the kitchen table putting her own slices of bread into the toaster, and warming her hands in the air above them as they cooked, as she did every single morning.

No. That morning was no different. Or, at least no different to me. While Bella's morning vegemite toast habit and her disdain for packed lunches gave some consistency to our lives, every day of living with Bella was a new experience. She was child. She was woman. She was manic energy, sloth, dancer, phone addict, insomniac, guitar strummer, high achiever, low achiever.

At sixteen. Bella turned adolescence into an art form.

And I lost her.

That day I lost her, I came home form work at the usual time, about a quarter to six. It was still light. I always rush home from work. I drive my car into the city and I pay exorbitant parking rates so that I can start my journey home to Bella the minute I finish work. No drinks after work. No hanging about for a gossip, or as we say in the public relations section, for a debrief. No staying late to impress the boss about my high levels of commitment. No. I put my head down and get on with it. I fit my overtime into an intense nine to five.

As soon after five as I can manage it, I throw my diary and a few files into my brief case, grab my car keys and dash to the lift, tapping my foot as the rows of red lights show me all the lifts which are above the twelfth floor or below it. I grimace as the lift mindlessly repeats its electronic message about having a nice day and when I am released, I click, click, click in my leather work shoes over the wide expanse of granite flooring and out the glass double doors. I dash across six lanes of crawling traffic to the underground car park and curve my way back up to the road. Shamelessly I dredge up all my aggressive driving tricks as I duck between lanes. The five pm news fades out on the car radio with the All Ordinaries Index and the overseas exchange rates on the Australian dollar. I have given up telling the radio this is useless information. It takes no notice.

The current affairs program entertains the listening part of my mind, while the automatic part clicks into its compulsive behaviour of counting traffic lights. Some other corner of my brain does the driving and the rest checks whether I need to shop on the way home. My single mother, working mother guilt does not let me stop for anything but the bare essentials, whatever they are. This guilt has laid low all day, but now it kicks in double time, with the thought of Bella, already home from school and by herself for at least an hour, except, of course, when she has after school sport, or music, or drops in to a friend's house on the way home.

My work friends give me such a bad time about rushing home to Bella. No, I tell them, time and time again, I can't do meetings at 5.30, I have to get home. I have a child. I'm a single Mum, you know. You lot wouldn't understand. Just wait until you have kids. OK, so she's a teenager. But look, she's home all by herself. I would mutter my explanations which were no explanation to them.

Twitters. Exchanges of knowing looks.

My morning fantasy of good mother pops up at various times during a bad day. Here I am, pulling the tray of biscuits out of the oven as Bella comes skipping through the open door of the house. The mother, who is there to listen about her day at school, who has tidied up the house and brought the clothes in from the line while they still smell of the sun and aren't the slightest bit damp.

But I can't do that image very often. Being that kind of mother would drive me crazy. It did drive me crazy as soon as Bella started pre-school so that I had to find my self respect and dust it off and fight my way back to work.

It would drive Bella crazy too. She doesn't want me picking up after her, hanging about for the perfect moment to catch her between her phone calls.

So why do I rush home? Well I guess it's my need, not Bella's, especially in the winter. I hate getting home after dark. Dark is when it should all be done by. Front door shut and dinner on the table. When I think about it, with honesty, this manic drive through the afternoon peak traffic is no different from the way I run the rest of my life. I want to be home, but not home all day. I want a real relationship with a man, but I don't want to live with one. Not yet. I want to keep seeing Geoff but I feel dreadful about his wife and kids. I want to work but I don't want to be doing the same old thing day after day. I want to save up for a holiday but I can't say no to most of what Bella asks for, or for what I ask for, for that matter. I want to be thin and I want to eat. I want to be fit and I just want to lie around most of the weekend. I don't want to give myself such a hard time but why is my life so fucking difficult?

But that day, exactly one week ago, I drove home from work as usual, and as soon as I put my key in the front door, I felt the emptiness of the house. Its emptiness entered my body, leaving a damp cold space. I shuddered as I took the shopping into the kitchen. I unlocked the back door and brought in the clothes, slightly damp as usual. I dumped the basket in the laundry. I went back into the kitchen and put on the kettle. I dragged myself upstairs and peeled off my work clothes and pulled on the sloppy tee shirt and tights from the chair next to my bed. I went back down into the kitchen, turned off the whistling kettle, made myself a pot of tea and sat down at the kitchen table.

I glanced over to the answering machine next to the phone. No blinking light. No messages. I sighed. Something was wrong. Something was very different. Something was missing. I knew nothing and I knew everything.

OK, I said to myself. OK Gina, just get it all together now. Turn on the radio. A bit of the old classical FM. That's better.

Turn it up. Yeah. Fold laundry, take basket upstairs to the landing. Put away shopping. Put away breakfast dishes. Start dinner. Yeah.

I told myself I have until seven o'clock before I started worrying. But I was already worrying. Where was she? I checked the wall calendar again. I could hardly read it. There was so little room in each of those squares. There were arrows pointing to notes in the margins. There were notes scratched out and more notes written on top. Some of the writing was too small. I peered close trying to work it out. It was Wednesday 17th May. I could remember that much from work. The space in the 17 box was filled in with scribble – hers and mine. But, look, the "at Andrew's" was joined by a wavy line to "band practice" from the square before, and I remembered that she did go to Andrew's the day before, because she came home tired out from lugging her guitar case and said that next time she might just do flute instead. And there was something else written there. But it was only my writing and it was a note to remind me to confirm my air tickets if I wanted to go away with Geoff for the weekend that Bella was due to spend with her father next month, but I had scratched out that note myself, because, well, it doesn't really matter why. Except that deep down I knew that Geoff needed to sort things out one way or another with Anna before I can really go away with him and enjoy it..

So it was empty. That day's box had nothing in it after all. OK, I told myself. We both stuff up. Bell and me. Sometimes she forgets to put things up on the calendar, and sometimes I forget too. But I did not convince myself. Not at all.

Fear. Remember fear? Yes I remembered that lump of lead that plummets down, down to the pit of my stomach? I remembered the damp crawling over my skin. I remembered the smell of it on my body. I remembered it in Peter's eyes when I said that I had to get out. I remembered that fear, hanging in the air between our two astonished faces when he said, 'So go. So get out.'

I remembered that fear, and I recognised it that day. I raised my arm to my nose and I could smell it. I wanted to scream, 'No, this is too hard!'

I looked up Miranda's phone number. I made myself dial it. I talked to her Father. I gave the first warning, the first sign that all was far from well in our little household. The telephone conversation followed, almost to the word, the one that had been running in my head. No, Bella wasn't there. No, they hadn't seen her all afternoon. Yes, he'd just check with Miranda. No, Miranda hadn't seen her since school got out. No, Miranda hadn't caught the bus. Meredith had picked her up and they'd gone to the dentist. Look, Gina, perhaps I'd better come over. I can come straight away if you like.

I allowed myself one tiny pang of guilt about not having taken Bella to the dentist for over a year.

Yeah. Thanks. I guess I'm not really alright. Have your dinner first. But yeah, thanks, come by in about an hour and I'll do some more phoning around.

Looking back, that night was the worst. Miranda's dad, Guy, tried very hard to be helpful. We sat down and he started the lists. The first one was all the people Bella might have gone to see, gone out with, wanted to be with. The second list was all the people whom she might have said something to, about tonight, about not coming home. The third list was other contacts in her life, through music, through going on the same school bus, through staying over at her Dad's house, friends she hadn't seen for a while, friends of mine she got on well with. We became totally focussed on these lists. I hung these lists on the fridge, some with phone numbers, some with emails, some just names.

Guy said we should start on the first list. So, one by one, we phone them. One by one, we drew a blank but we didn't leave blanks. Oh no. We left Peter, my ex, hysterical and accusing. We left my brother Teff concerned and wanting to mount a full scale police inquiry.

We left trails of anguish with my friends, with the parents of Bella's friends, and when it was too late at night to worry any more people, we went around to the police. The young officer on duty, was polite enough, but he said we shouldn't take it too seriously if she didn't come home that night. He said we would be surprised how many teenagers stay away one or even a few nights, leaving their parents in a panic. To the police, missing wasn't missing until it was at least forty eight hours old. He said I should keep making lists.

I didn't sleep at all that night. By morning I had pages full of lists with as many contact details as I could find in my phone, my address book, my email lists, my head.

I needed to go to work. I took a photo of Bella with me. I scanned it into my computer. I worked it into a poster. Shamelessly I printed off 100 copies, using expensive coloured paper. Over the next few evenings, I put them in shops, on walls, near our home, near her school, everywhere I could think of. I phoned back our friends and relatives on the 'A' list and emailed them a poster to put up, anywhere, everywhere.

Now, a week down the track, I vent all my frustration and grief on bothering the police. Every day before work and then again after work, I call in at the local police station. I demand to know what they have done. I demand to see the evidence of their actions to date. I want to know what they intend to do. When? How? And then what? They have lots of statistics to comfort me with, like how many teenagers are reported missing in NSW every day, like how many return home after one night, three nights, one week. I am sure they also have statistics on how many teenagers are abducted and raped and murdered, but they don't trot those out.

At last the police are beginning to take Bella's disappearance seriously although they still talk about her as having run away. At one level, I find the subtle changes in them reassuring, at another I find it terrifying. I have filled in a missing person's report. I have left some of the posters with the police. They are making suggestions, like I should try and think of reasons why Bella might have left home. Sometimes, when they are being patient with me, I want to stay there and watch while they do things to find her. But I know that as soon as I leave, they get on with their crises for the day. When they are condescending to me I want to smash their faces in. I am following up on one of the police's rare suggestions. I phone Telstra and ask for a print out of the phone numbers to my home over the past three months. I have a long altercation with someone called Charles, and ask to be put through to his manager, who is someone called Simone, and I explain to her once more that, yes, I know I get this information with my phone bill but I can't seem to find the last one and anyway I want the most recent three months and I want them now. Somehow I don't want to tell the Telstra people that the police suggested this because my darling Bella has gone missing because I so do not like Charles and Simone it is none of their business.

To my shame, instead, I just cry and blubber and repeat over and over I want them now. It works. Simone asks if I would like the information emailed immediately. I back down with an ingratiating thank you so much, Simone, thank you so much.

Apart from my twice daily visits to interrogate the police, I am detached. My body gets out of bed, showers, makes coffee, drives to work. It gets through the day, answers the phone, writes drafts, walks around the city at lunch time. My body eats take-aways as it plonks itself down in front of TV at night, watches whatever, listens to the incoming phone calls through the answering machine. I hear friends checking in to see if I'm alright. No, I scream to the machine, I am not alright. People with unfamiliar voices leave names I do not recognise, till I realise they are the parents of Bella's friends, her teachers, her music teacher. I hit the erase button. All gone.

Bella's father Peter has taken to dropping over after he's had dinner with his new family. I know he does not want to be here but he wants to be at home even less. So he wanders in about nine and fiddles with the remote of the television. My brother Teff has also taken to dropping in about the same time. He and Peter have always got on. I could never see what they had in common. Now they sit and chat a bit while Peter flips the channels. Teff does not go insane at this behaviour. He understands that this is what Peter needs to do. I get them cups of coffee and go up to bed, leaving them to let themselves out, whenever. I half hear their voices from the room below, and drift in and out of the lightest of sleep with the radio on for comfort. Anything but the silence. Silence is the window for thoughts that need to be shut out.

Silence brings images before my eyes whether they are shut or open. Silence makes me cry. I repeat the mantra that I must hold myself together, but I have no idea for what. I do not give in.

Except when I see Alma. Once a week I sit curled up in the big floppy arm chair facing Alma, my therapist. Last Friday, as I worked my way through the square box of tissues on the white cane table between us, Alma gently, and not so gently, led me out of numbness and into the terrifying world of feelings. Alma is very good at this. She leads and I follow. She and I have had months of practice.

Last night, when Peter and Teff were over, we printed off the Telstra email with all the phone numbers. I was amazed how much phoning in and out Bella and I can do in 12 weeks, well mostly Bella.

I got my lists from the fridge door and together we tried to match more phone numbers to names. It took hours. Teff had the most recent sheets and he picked up that there were phone ins from public phone boxes. They certainly weren't my calls. I promised I would take this to the police in the morning.

My rational mind keeps telling me that Bella is not dead. I know that there are thousand of run-away teenagers in this city. I know that, whatever her reasons are, Bella is not running away from anything. I know that there is nothing in her life that is so horrible, so scary that it is making her run away. If she has run, then she must be running away to someone, to do something, for some reason that I don't know about. My rational mind is little comfort to me now. It can reason away as long as it likes, I am scared.

The hardest thing is not knowing where she is. The second hardest thing is not knowing why she has run away. And the third hardest thing is the fear I detect in other people – their fear that she is dead. I see it in their faces. I stay away from those people.

Alma is helping me look at the loss. Actually, Alma has been helping me deal with loss for almost a year now. Loss is something I seem to specialise in. I can count the main losses which make big holes inside me. The loss of my mother and the loss of the mother I would have much preferred. The loss of my father whom I hardly ever saw and who did not want to know me. The loss of childhood or the childhood that I wanted – with fun, and other kids running around the house, and two parents who were young and alive.

But now I need Alma to help me with losing Bella. The others have been dry runs for this loss. This is the big mother of all losses. I feel overwhelming shame that I have lost her. That I have been honoured with the gift of this extraordinary child and I don't deserve it. My shame is about not noticing the tell-tale signs. My shame is about being too busy or distracted with my own life to notice that she was in some sort of crisis. How can a mother live with her own child and not be 'there' enough for her?

And now she is somewhere else. Gone.

2. THE VOLVOX

It is now two weeks since she left. I race home from work as usual. I cling to my compulsive routine and habits. They comfort me. Besides, I might need them again in the future. If or when she comes home. I leave work at the same time I always did. I take the same route home. I count the number of traffic lights like I always do, greens and reds separately, so that I know whether it was a good trip or not. Sometimes ABC radio distracts me. I miss one or two sets. The total doesn't tally as I park in front of my house. This makes it a bad trip, even worse than lots of red lights.

I let myself into the house. I quickly check around for any signs of change. Has the lounge seat opposite the TV been sat it? Any apple cores on the coffee table? A kicked off shoe? Any smells of school bag. None. I set the timer on the oven for an hour. I allow myself this time every day now, hiding away in her bedroom.

I climb up to the attic, hauling my body up the ladder, and I flop down on Bella's bed, exhausted. I'm not sleeping properly. I'm not eating properly. I have gone back to smoking joints. My body is a mess.

But her little room is becoming a sanctuary for me. This little room high up in the roof. I acknowledge the role reversal as I the mother crawl into my Bella's private space.

I lie on my back on her bed. I close my eyes and conjure up her face in my mind. All I can see is her face in the poster I have been putting up. Her other self, the laughing playful moody Bella is fading. How can this be?

This attic room is so tiny. It is like crawling up into a play tent. First you have to climb the stairs to the landing outside the spare room and then you have to climb up a ladder into a square hole in the ceiling. And then you emerge up through the floor, into Bella's attic. The room feels even smaller as the walls slope in on two sides leaving a little strip in the middle where you can stand up straight. All the furniture is placed against the two walls which do not slope. The bed runs along one wall, and on the other there is just enough space for a narrow chest of drawers and an open wooden rack that her clothes hang from in a tangled mess. There are windows in each of the sloping walls. One side looks out over the back lane and you can see the rows of little gardens on either side of the lane. The opposite windows look out over roof tops and, if you lean right out of the window you can see the street.

But mostly you can see sky. Especially if you lie or sit on the bed.

This attic room is uncontaminated by her school things which have been banished to the spare bedroom, ensuring that it is never spare. Not with her desk there, and all her school books spread out over the floor. Her CDs form a pile beneath the stereo. Her sports paraphernalia forms a layer over the bed half covering the pile of stuffed animals, the guitar and the sheets of music.

I like the small scale of this house. It comforts me. Everything that I need and want is in easy reach. I can plant one foot in the kitchen and by turning around I can reach every bit of bench space. I keep my possessions pruned down to a minimum. Just enough. I hate too much. I used to hate all the unused stuff that Peter and I managed to gather over the years. Of course Bella's stuff is out of control, but that does not bother me. These two rooms are her territory. My bedroom is mine and the lounge room, well, I am a bit of a junk nazi. It has to stay minimalist.

I think of my primary school friend Sally whose grandparents lived just a few houses down the street from here. I used to go there with her, sometimes, on Saturday afternoons. It was an "original" Paddington terrace. Her grandparents had no intention of selling it to the developers or trendies. It had been their home since they were first married. Sally's mum and her four brothers and sister grew up in that tiny two bedroom house. One bedroom for the parents with the two girls sleeping on the narrow verandah which led off this room and almost hung over the footpath. Bunks for the four boys in the second bedroom. I think of them now and wonder where did they put their stuff? How did you get six children off to school every day in clean clothes when there was no room for clothes, no dryer for the weeks of wet weather? I wonder if they had toys? Games? Bikes? Friends? I never thought to ask Sally's mother or grandparents these important questions when I was a child. I just thought Sally was so lucky to have a grandmother who baked biscuits which smelt of peanut butter and had little fork marks across the top. And lucky to have a grandfather who pretended he could never remember her name and made her giggle every single time with the silly names he made up.

I wonder why I think about this now. Somehow it is comforting to remember this suburb how it was when I was Bella's age or even younger. I like to go back even further in my mind, and think about Paddington in the depression with large families in tiny houses, and dads off work and then mums and kids by themselves when dads were at the war, and the terrible time after, when the war damaged dads came home. And I can see the narrow streets full of kids playing cricket and riding billy carts. I can hear the frenzied drinking at the local pubs just before the barman shouted "Time's up gentlemen" at six o'clock in the afternoon.

I think about tensions boiling in these little houses, and girls like Sally's mum doing nursing so that she could leave home, and her older brothers leaving home as teenagers to be jackaroos in the country, and I think about the domestic violence thumps and bumps and muffled screams clearly heard in the next room or the next house, and I think of these women who had no way out for themselves and their children.

And sometimes, late at night, in that state between sleep and awake, I can almost feel this house's memory of its families eking out their squashed existence within these tiny walls.

But lying here now, I feel this little room in the roof space strangely comforting. When I look across to the wall at the foot of the bed, I can see the framed drawing Bella did when she was 12, when she was in her first year of high school. She so wanted to please Miss Cameron, her young science teacher who looked like Madonna and who had the whole class searching for the strangest living creatures they could find, and then drawing them with captions.

I framed Bella's. It was so beautiful. I wanted to hang it on the landing of the stairs so that we could see it as we went up to our bedrooms. But Bella had hung it here and here it stayed.

It is a microscopic green hollow ball made up of tiny one celled organisms, each with its pair of hair-thin flagella facing outwards, waving in the water. The caption says 'We are a volvox. We are one.'

I focus on the volvox, seeing all the little cells living together, swimming together, sharing the food, making babies together, protecting them in the hollow of the sphere until they are big enough to take their place in the outside world. My eyes begin to close and I can see the volvox rotating fast in the water, human faces on the tip of each little cell, long arms waving in pairs in the clear water. I see my mother's face, and my brother Teff's face and the face of my father Alberto whose face is etched deep with sadness and whose eyes, even in my wildest imagination, never make contact with mine. And I see the faces of all my father's Italian family from the big house in the mountains. I see Peter's face, and his new wife and her little boy. I see Geoff and the faces of his children from the tiny square in his wallet. And I feel a huge wave of sadness beginning tight in my chest and welling up and rushing over me. Oh Mama, I feel so alone. I feel my loneliness, I feel loneliness embedded in this old house, in this city, in this world, and a great big universal loneliness engulfs me. So many single people living out their single lives.

Sergeant Pepper's creeps into my head. All the lonely people. Where do they come from?

And for the first time I wonder if Bella was drawn to the volvox because she felt alone. Because she felt deprived of a full family life, the big extended tribe, just like I did, when I was her age. When I was growing up with my mum. Just the boring two of us, after my older brother left home.

I lie on Bella's bed and half close my eyes. That picture. I cannot stop looking at my volvox. I need to reassure myself. I need to count. Apart from Bella, I have Teff. Who else? Friends, OK. What friends? Do I have a protective sphere of friends? A circle even? A semicircle? An arc? Stop, I tell myself. This is pathetic. OK.

OK. I sigh. What friends?

My work friends. My mind wanders round the office. The people I stop to chat to. The people I have sometimes have lunch with. The people I confide in, well, at least about how I feel about work. Yep, work friends. Nothing special there.

Suddenly I have this immense yearning to be back in my 16 year old body hanging out week in, week out, with my real friends. After school. Before school. Days in between school. We stretch out on the grass, looking up at trees and clouds. We stretch out on the hill above the beach, listening to the waves. We stretch across each others arms and legs and beds, listening to music and fantasising about boys. We wear each other's clothes and dreams. We walk miles, arms linked. We sob together in dark movie houses. Amy and Cassie and Gina. We knew each other better than each of us knew ourselves.

Not any more. I've lost contact. Amy moved away and I never see Cassie. She moves in a different circle. And the difference is money.

But I do have friends. I have the friends we made, Peter and I, when we were young and when Bella was little. Especially the ones who are alone, like me. Yes, I do see Ella from Carl and Ella, and Deb from Deb and Dave and I see Ron from Lisa and Ron.

Now I can name more. There's my lover Geoff and sometimes we go out with his friends. There are other people I have over for a meal. People I go away with on weekends. People I go to the movies with. People I phone for a chat.

But not a circle. No. No way my circle. I just seem to dip in and out of their circles, every now and again.

I sit with this for a while. This new insight. A circle breaker, circuit breaker. And I wonder if I have chosen this so that I don't get too close, too closed in, too closed off. I wonder if I need my escape routes. I wonder if I have the ability to get in, but not too in, and to keep out, but not too out.

And perhaps that's how I've been with lovers. Not too committed eh? Moving out of their circle when it gets a bit too serious. Getting back in touch with being single again. And then getting out of touch with it. Again.

I get up and turn Bella's volvox to the wall. Fucking thing! What would it know, anyway?

I must have fallen asleep for a while. For it is dark. I panic. For a minute I am totally confused. I am lying still stretched out on Bella's bed and I try to steady myself by breathing deeply, remembering the voice of Sasha, my yoga teacher from way back. Breathe in through the nose. Feel the back ribs expanding. Feel the diaphragm lowering. Feel the abdomen filling out. Slowly exhale though the mouth. Feel the tension in the spine reeeeelax.

Suddenly I sit bolt upright. I can smell lavender oil as if Bella were there in the room with me. I keep breathing with rapt concentration, as if the smell will disappear if I stop for one second taking deep breaths in through my nose. I wonder how on earth I could have missed it before and spare a thought of forgiveness of myself for being in such a mess I can't even smell the most important thing in the world.

I start searching the room for clues, nose sniffing and twitching. Nothing. I turn the pillow over in disgust before I can flop back on it I notice damp patches on the down side of the pillow slip. I put my finger to the damp spots and put my finger in my mouth. Salt. Tears. I know that without a doubt Bella has been here today. She must still have her key. She has let herself into the house. She has lain down on her bed and had a good cry and left the smell of lavender oil lingering. I start trembling. She is alive and she is near.

I breathe deeply and instantly Bella returns to my mind. I can smell her perfume. I can smell her lavender oil. She never lets herself run out and she dabs it onto her forehead and neck every single day.

The rest of the week is a right-off. Wednesday, no teary pillow. Thursday. I see Alma. I can't concentrate. It is a frightful session. Friday. I try to stay out most of Saturday. Sunday. On Sunday night I long for Tuesday. I remember Bella was born on a Tuesday. 'Tuesday's child is ....' What the hell is Tuesday's child? What the hell does it matter?

But I am hooked on Tuesday. I am convinced she will come again. It makes sense to my addled mind that this is the beginning of a pattern.

The night before Tuesday is the big one for me. I remember that song about hating Mondays. So I have arranged to so something on Monday nights. I go walking with Terry.

I had been aware of Terry living in the terrace house opposite mine since he moved in about a year ago. Sometimes I would see him as he left home in the morning. We would both come out our front doors at the same time. Nod at each other and smile. He, calm and unhurried. Me, dashing across the nature strip to my car, skirt, shirt, scarf whatever flying behind, attached at weird angles to my body.

For some reason I thought Terry was an architect, or something else that was angular. Like him. Covert glances through his open front door in the summer heat showed a sparse house inside, to match the sparse outside. He had an angular dog with a square head and a square little body. Terry would often walk his dog at night, on a leash, and the dog would obediently trot beside Terry's even pace, set by his long legs.

Over the year, Terry has been put on a shelf in my mind. There has been no space for him while I have been rushing in circles to get to work, get home from work, keep tabs on Bella, see friends, start and stop exercise programs and be on and off again with Geoff. Perhaps I wrote him off as boring. And anyway, I hate dogs. And perhaps he's gay.

But since Bella has gone, I have become much more aware of Terry's presence. I noticed his light on when I turned my bedroom light off. I wake up sometimes, hours later and notice that his light is still on. Does he fall asleep, sometimes, with it on? Stupid. He's an insomniac, like just about everyone else I know. His curtains are drawn, and my curtains too, but I can still see the glow of his light through the crack where my curtains don't quite meet. His do meet, of course.

But since Bella has gone, I sense it more, that he is there, all alone in the main bedroom of his little terrace, and there am I all alone in the main bedroom of mine, and lately, I feel so lonely that I ache. I ache in my chest and in my stomach. My legs are restless and won't lie still. I feel prickles of tears behind my eyes and I get so cross at myself for being so pathetic. For feeling like a victim. And it doesn't matter how much I tell myself that I am supposed to be the adult around here, I often feel like a very small child.

I give myself a few moments to wonder what life would be like, if I still lived with Peter, long after we stopped loving each other. I also allow a few moments of being really assertive with Geoff instead of being so fucking understanding about how difficult it is for him to tell his wife that I exist. But perhaps his procrastination suits me. I can just hang in there, not having to face whether I really want to spend the rest of my life with this guy. I could be going out at night to bars with my single women friends and I could stop knocking back all those hands that reach out to me with genuine love and kindness. Couples saying, come over for dinner tonight, we have an extra ticket for the Brahms concert at the Opera House, and you never drop in anymore, like you used to when the kids were little. And I could do a bit of reaching out myself instead of staying at home, giving myself such a bad time for being a mess because Bella has gone. And, a little voice whispers that, let's face it, I was a mess before Bella even left.

So it's really easy to lie in bed in the dark, looking across at the glow from the bedroom across the street, and wonder what's with Terry? What is he reading? Why don't I see people visiting him for sleepovers – no women, no men. Is this all he's got, the few cars that pull up, the few singles and couples that enter his house, smartly dressed, bringing bottles of wine. They knock at his door and go through and stay in his house for a few hours. But what else? And does he look across the road and realise that precious few people have been passing in and out of my house of the past few weeks.

Then, last Saturday morning, Terry knocked at my door. I had got up early for a walk, picked up the weekend newspapers, made myself breakfast and taken the lot back to bed, pretending I had woken up in my tracksuit and that someone had brought me the papers and breakfast on a tray. It was snug under the covers on that cold morning. Surprisingly, I was having a nice time.

Reluctantly I shouted out 'coming', leapt out of bed, uncrumpled my tracksuit as best I could, dragged the brush through my hair, bounded down the stairs and opened the door. There was Terry.

He smiled. He said, 'Hi Gina. I heard about Bella being missing a while ago. Thought I'd just come over and say, well, say that I'm really sorry. It must be very hard, for you, just now.' He handed me a small package and said,

'If you don't use it you can always give it back'.

I started to open the package, but stopped when I realised it was a plastic bag of heads and a packet of papers. We both smiled.

I asked him in, but he stayed on the door mat. I told him I was really touched. I was. I told him that yes, it was really hard. I wanted to tell him that she was contacting me in her own way, but I couldn't. I didn't want to frighten him off.

So we stood there, with Terry giving the impression he wanted to stay and talk and me giving the impression that it was nice to have him on my front door mat. It was. And just as he turned to go, I blurted out,

'Hey Terry. Perhaps I could come for a walk some evenings. With your dog. Would you mind that?'

And he said that he wouldn't mind that at all, and that, in fact, he would welcome some company as his dog wasn't much of a talker.

'How about Monday?' And he said, 'How about 8 o'clock? See you then.'

And I said 'Goodoh' and shut the door and went inside and went back to bed to have a think about what I had just done.

Nothing. I said to myself. Gina, you have done nothing. You are going to join Terry and his dog for a walk, one walk, on Monday night. If you don't like it, then no more walks with Terry and his dog. If you do like it, more walks. OK?

OK, I told myself. OK. But I hate dogs.

So, Monday night I walked with Terry and it was just fine.

When I got home, I plonked down in front of the telly flipping through the channels. I was so agitated and exhausted. I tried to have a read, then started to make a list of the things that were going through my head. I failed on both fronts.

Finally I climbed up into her room. Then I climbed down again. I changed my sheets. I put on a wash. I went to bed. I turned the bedside light off and the radio on. I turned the light on and the radio off. I finally fell asleep with the light on.

Tuesday morning I left an envelope under her pillow before I go to work.

Inside was a simple note.

'Darling Bella, I love you, Mum.' and two $50 notes.

3. THE ENVELOPE

This is the third week and I am obsessed with what is under her pillow. My focus has gone off the police although I stop in every day or so, just in case. I am not so intense with them, and the Paddington police must be rejoicing.

It won't leave me alone. I think about it while I'm driving, at my desk, drinking coffee. My anxious state is at its worst today, this Tuesday,

Paul, my supervisor at work is unaware of the tangled mess my brain has become. He gives me detailed instructions about a pamphlet he wants me to design for respite carers of disabled children. I watch with fascination as Paul's mouth makes different shapes and I hear the monotonous drone of his voice. I nod in agreement to his ideas. I even make a few suggestions myself, which I then put under Bella's pillow.

As soon as I go back to my desk I can remember nothing. I have absolutely no idea what he said, what I said, or what I have agreed to do. I hum a few bars of 'Yesterday' over and over again as I sit at my desk and look at my screen saver.

Today, my brain is chewing, gnawing, teasing with a great big mass of tangled questions which occupy my whole head space. These questions live in my brain. They tumble around. They get themselves into knots. I could start with any one of the dozens of threads handing out. Hanging onto the comfort of my screen saver, I grab a big one.

Was leaving out money a really crass thing to do? Is that all she thinks she is to me? One hundred dollars? Is it enough for her immediate needs? Is it so mean she won't bother coming back? Is it too much?

I start doing sums. $100 a week is $14.57 per day. If she only has to feed herself she can just manage on that, but there would be little left over for extras. If she is contributing to rent and still has to buy food then, no way.

I start wondering about how she is living, day to day? Is she sleeping in one of those large dark warehouses with the boarded up windows and blackened, chipped, seat-less toilets which are not even connected? Is she with other street kids in filthy squats? Does she have any of her friends with her? Do they use drugs? Do they sell drugs? Do they sell their bodies? What does she eat? Where does she wash? Does she have a pillow? What does she do when she has run out of clean undies? Does she go to bed hungry?

Hungry? Did I check the fridge last Tuesday to see if something was missing?

Should I have left out some of her favourite spinach pie? Baskets of fruit? Do I want her to come home and drag off loads of food to share with those drugged out, sore-covered, runny-nosed, smelly-fanny kids? How the fuck am I supposed to know the rules?

I spend the rest of this day at work going over in my mind, last night's walk with Terry.

This was my first walk with Terry and Bounce. That's his dog. Bounce.

We walked and talked and walked and didn't talk. Either seemed OK.

I am surprised at how easy it was, with Terry. Despite my resolves not to do too much talking and to find out more about Terry, as usual, I end up talking about me. Someone once said to beware of women who live alone as they talk too much, and perhaps I'm getting like that. But then, I've always talked too much.

Terry is a good listener. Mostly he asked about my job, and that is easy and unthreatening to talk about so I told him about working in the public relations area of the welfare department and how I have to make up pamphlets and posters and deal with the media. I told him that there used to be a whole section of us, but since the government cutbacks a few years ago, now there is just me. I told him they left me here because they think I have a good overall knowledge of what the department does but that this is far from the truth. I have to ask people all the time what they do. I have to ask them how they do it. I get them to take me with them to visit clients or case conferences or other agencies so that I have some idea what to write about.

He said he thought it sounded interesting. I don't have the heart to tell him I think I outgrew the job about three years ago.

Then he talked a bit about what he does. Well I was wrong. He's not an architect or anything like it. He is an academic and teaches history at the university. He said he never set out to be an academic. He said he wonders what on earth he thought he was going to do with a post graduate degree in history, other than teach history. He said he is not very good at planning his life.

I tell myself once again that it is good for me to have some-thing to do on Monday nights. They are such tense times for me, wondering if Bella is going to come home the next day, for a visit, or perhaps, dare I hope, for good. I didn't talk about Bella with Terry. I can't trust that yet. I cry so easily. I don't want to spoil making a new friend by getting all wet, right at the beginning. So we skirted around the real stuff. We didn't talk about why he lives by himself either. I do wonder about his history, like why history, and his insomnia, like why. But all I was left with was his passion with the conflicts in Ireland. And tough as it must be in Northern Ireland, it is a fairly safe thing to be passionate about especially here in Sydney.

I didn't get very far with Bounce. She and I have developed a mutual pretending the other is not there. She certainly had no trouble pretending that I am not there. She got me pigeonholed as a non-dog person from day 1. I don't understand dogs. I don't see the point in talking to them. I turned my head so that I didn't notice when the inevitable plastic bag expertly inverted on Terry's hand enfolded the poo on the footpath or the grass verge and got sealed with a neat knot. Yuk.

I drive home this Tuesday. I park the car. And then I start running, front door key extended in line with the key hole. I'm inside! Up the stairs two, three at a time. I don't dare breathe. Up the ladder, I climb and haul myself into her room. I lunge at the pillow and tear it off her bed. The envelope is gone. In its place is a clover flower. One perfect tiny white ball of a flower on a thin green stalk. Laughing and crying I race down the ladder, into the bathroom, just make it to the toilet, pee, sob, laugh, warm liquids bubbling out of every hole.

Still sitting on the toilet, I start to plot how I can pretend to go to work next Tuesday and I see myself hiding behind the hedge of the building further down the other side of the street. All day I'm going to hide behind the hedge. Great. Or how about I creep back inside the house and hide under my bed. Sure. Or how about I change the "I love you" note to asking if we can see each other at a given time, at the beach or in a cafe or library or something. Now this has possibilities for me. I go downstairs. I could have at least an hour of planning this one. Or how about I just trust it. Sometimes the thought slips into what is left of my brain, that it is not really Bella who has come. Just someone who uses Tasmanian Lavender Oil and who has a key to our house.

Someone who ripped these things off Bella and forced her at gunpoint to divulge her address.

No. It is Bella. And then I worry that by giving her money I am helping her stay away. That's right. What mother could be so dumb she actually pays her run-away kid a weekly allowance? But I cannot bear to think of her being cold and hungry. One hundred dollars won't be enough for somewhere to live. Not in Sydney. But it might just feed her.

I owe it to my mother to make sure Bella is as safe as possible. She told me often enough that she did not escape the gas chambers of Europe so that I could fritter away my life. I can hear her voice now telling me that she did not do all that suffering so that her namesake granddaughter had to walk the streets of Sydney cold and hungry.

I owe it to my mother? I brush my mother away. I do not owe.

I go back up to Bella's room. I lie down on her bed again, on this Tuesday evening, enjoying the fresh wafts of lavender. I spin the tiny clover flower between my fingers. It is so precious. It is so tenuous, this contact between us.

I am feeling much calmer now. I know she is alive. I know she is in Sydney, at least on Tuesdays. I allow myself the luxury of closing my eyes and feeling my body melt into her bed. And I can see Bella, my beautiful teenage daughter plummeting backwards through time to that tiny scrawny underweight little baby with the face of an angel, held tight in my arms in the maternity ward.

'So, it's all settled,' Peter says. 'We'll call her Katelin.'

I start to cry. Again.

'What is it now?' he asks, a slight edge of exasperation in his voice. Peter is as new to all of this as I am. And he is getting a bit tetchy. Peter likes to plan ahead and then have everything go to plan. Well it hasn't gone to plan at all. Our baby came five weeks early so that instead of being at the beginning of his holidays, the birth has come in the middle of a very important contract. I am supposed to be glowing, gracious and confident. And I'm not. I'm pathetic. My breasts hurt, I'm constipated and my baby keeps getting lighter instead of heavier. I think she will disappear before I have a chance to get her home.

The nurses, who look either like teenagers or old prunes, tell me that babies who are a bit on the small side often lose weight. This makes no sense to me at all. Perhaps I should have had a bigger one to start off with but I can't help feeling that I didn't have too many choices about all of this. I also think my baby is turning yellow and I can't imagine why no one else has noticed. Do I wait for them to notice? Or could I have got a slightly Asian sperm to begin with? Do Asian babies start off pink and then slowly turn yellow? Who do you ask about that sort of thing?

'I want to call her Bella.' I finally get it out. Peter looks at me with amazement.

'But we discussed it. We decided on Katelin.'

I can remember we discussed it. I'm not a total moron. I can remember Peter setting the night, in his diary, and marking the date on the calendar on the fridge. I can remember him arriving home with three books of names from the library. And it was good fun, deciding we wanted something a bit European sounding, a bit different, but a name which could be shortened to something which sounded quite ordinary if it were that kind of kid. Like Stefan, my brother's name. Still Teff to me after all these years. But definitely Stevo when he was in high school and desperately trying to make the first grade football team.

I knew I wasn't playing fair. I was reneging on a well thought out, well planned, joint decision which I had made while in sound mind and body.

Well I didn't feel too sound in mind or body. I started talking to Peter through my pathetic sobs. What I really wanted to say was, 'I want to call her after my mother.'

But I must have said, 'I want my mother.'

Peter turned on his heel and walked out, shaking his head in disbelief. My mother had been dead for well over two years.

'Bella, Bella, Bella, Bella'. I say the name out loud now, and I smile as I recall my first act of defiance towards Peter. I smile even more at the memory that it was the first of many.

'Tell me about my grandma Bella'. I hear her voice through my day dreams. I hear her voice in this little room as plain as if her body were there as well, but I know that if I look there will be no body there and perhaps even the act of looking will make the voice disappear. So I conjure up her sixteen year old face, almost a perfect oval, her straight nose, her wide mouth and her lovely big dark eyes. Her dark hair hangs down untidily past her shoulders, her fringe cutting off the top of the oval with a severe line. Her skin, almost translucent. Dark circles under her eyes which have always given me relentless pangs of guilt about letting her stay up too late, about not looking after her nutrition, about the state of her kidneys, or is it liver.

'Tell me about Grandma Bella. Tell me about when she was young, Mum.'

'I don't know very much about her when she was young. She never talked much about growing up in Germany or being a young girl before the war. From what your uncle Teff tells me she came from an old Berlin family and her parents had great plans for a career for her on the concert stage. She was a natural in music. I can still just remember sitting on her lap when I was little with her singing me to sleep with such a beautiful voice. I could feel my body tingle as the music vibrated through it. I thought it was magic, my mother's singing. I used to try to stay awake so I could keep feeling the sounds.'

'But when she was young, Mum.'

'She was Beulah then. A young German girl. A bit of a rebel from the little she told me. When she finished school she kept studying her piano and singing with the best teachers money could buy, and at night, she would sneak out and go to the music hall. She loved parties. The family lived in a big apartment block in the centre of the city, and lots of their relatives lived in the same block. She said that she could always find at least one aunty or uncle who would take her side, who would stand up for her when her parents tried to scold her.

But she got pregnant. She was only nineteen then. Teff's father was one of her admirers, not even a real boy-friend. He was an older man. He was a friend of her father who used to take her out dancing sometimes. Her parents thought she would be safe with him.'

'Go on.'

'Well, when she realised she was pregnant she became totally obsessed with leaving Germany. She begged her parents to take her somewhere out of Europe. She begged her grandparents, all the relatives, even the father of her child, whom she didn't even like very much. They all thought she was mad. And in a way she was. She could focus on only one thing. She had to leave.

Her father offered to arrange an abortion, but she begged him not to make her do it. She wanted the baby, but she had to go away. Bella helped herself to some of her mother's jewellery, sold it and got enough money to leave. All alone. Pregnant and nineteen years old. She caught a train to Amsterdam, and from there a boat to Australia. It was 1940. She never saw her family again. Or Teff's father. They were all killed by the Nazis.'

'Oh Mum, that is so sad.'

Yes.'

'And she was so brave.'

'Yes'

'I have to go now.'

I let her go. I lie there and think they are both brave, both my Bellas. I'm not.

I start playing a mind game which once started, has to run its course till the end – till my mother's death. I picture her at 20, alone in a new land, a maid in the home of wealthy Australian Jews, who are doing their bit for the war effort by taking in this very pregnant young Jewish refugee who speaks little English and who has never done anything that maids are supposed to do.

At 20 she gives birth to Teff, in a hospital, among strangers, and the family look after her till she is well enough to go back to her housework and cooking but she is very sad and misses her own family, and wants to spend all her days looking after her baby, who grows big and sturdy.

At 20 I dropped out after two years of university. I couldn't cope. I was failing my grades. Looking back I think I was probably depressed.

At 22 she answered an advertisement for a job with an Italian family who were running a guest house in the Blue Mountains, and despite the presence of little Teff, she told them that she would be able to cook and clean and even sing and play music for the guests.

At 22 I was backpacking around New Zealand. I didn't even make it all the way to Asia or Europe like most of my friends.

At 25 my mother started a long illicit affair with one of the Italian uncles – Alfredo, and she shared Alfredo with his wife Rosa, except that Rosa did not know that she was sharing Alfredo, the fun-loving naughty boy-man, the favourite son whom everyone loved and nobody chastised. He had one rule. No babies.

I smile as I think of my mother, now Bella, ensconced in the Roma Guest House with her beautiful young son, now Stefano, both getting more and more Italian as they years rolled on, in down town Katoomba. Dotted along the mountain ridges were other guest houses where the European Jews from Sydney spent their family holidays. But they might as well have been as far away as Europe itself for all the contact my mother had with her own people.

I spent my twenties, drifting, drifting, until I finally went back to university and finished my degree and met Peter. Peter planned and I drifted into marriage. I can't recall much in the way of romance. And although I am Jewish too, I can't recall too much in the way of being around Jews, either. At last, my mother and I have something in common.

I do hate being so obsessed with this game.

But after nearly two decades of blissful years my mother's life fell apart. The unthinkable happened. Just before her fortieth birthday she fell pregnant to Alfredo. Rosa, the desperately unhappy childless Rosa fell under a train as it was pulling into Katoomba station, breaking the triangular web which held my mother's life in place.

Alfredo could not bear to look at her. The family closed ranks. Alfredo retreated to alcohol and the four walls of his room. Once more my mother fled. Pregnant. Only this time she was no longer young and pretty. When I was nearly forty, my Bella had just started school and my mother Bella had been dead for seven years. It was cancer and it was very quick. At least she could stop wondering how she got such a wimp for a daughter.

I now tell myself the story as it should have been. I picture her in the big Italian family, in the big house with the garden of old camellia trees and azalea bushes, living out her middle and older years in comfort and surrounded by love, the smell of fresh coffee and vases of daffodils. Alfredo, relieved that Rosa had solved their huge dilemma, could not believe his luck at siring a child in his mature years and lavished my mother with attentiveness until, and indeed long after, she gave birth to their perfect daughter. They called her Gina.

Try as I might I cannot make that story stick. No. We moved out, in disgrace, my mother, her almost adult son and me, snugly unborn. We moved into a tiny flat in Bronte, near the sea. When I was a few weeks old, my mother put me into the care of a neighbour who had three of her own children, and went off to work.

I look back now and I can see my mother the survivor. A very special survivor.

At 40 my survival skills were not much at all to be proud of. My Bella had started school and I was a single mum, not as a result of a tragedy, but just because I no longer loved Peter, if, indeed, I ever did.

I often wonder about survivors. I seem to attract survivors into my life. My best friend at school, Sally, had survived rheumatic fever as a child and her legacy from those long hospital stays was a wonky heart. Geoff is a survivor of sorts. He survived a father who was alcoholic and beat the shit out of him. I wonder why I attract them. I wonder if I have something more to learn from them, as if I didn't have enough to learn from my own mother, the greatest survivor of all times.

And I wonder what is left, when they're through with all their surviving, what is left for them to give? And yes I can say that despite the endless sighs of disappointment from my own mother, when I think about it, I am so thankful that I am not real survivor material.

My survivor mum had her own cafe well and truly running by the time she was forty five. She kept me strong and healthy. My teeth were checked every six months. My feet grew straight and strong in the best leather school shoes. My fingers were trained to run every scale the piano knew. I had the right toys for playing in the street after school – a bicycle and roller blades. And every night she sat on the end of my bed and we talked about my day, my fears, my scarce moments of gain and fame, my failures to understand the politics of the girls' playground, my dreams, my goals, my crushes. Sometimes she would sing me to sleep. But even as a child I knew that only half of her was ever there, on the end of the bed. The other half was work-ing, planning, calculating, budgeting, making up new menus, redecorating the cafe.

By the time I was the age my Bella is now, my mother had just fifteen years left, six with me at home and then nine more by herself. I have finished. She is dead. So can I stop now?

No. There is more. When I was conceived, Teff was getting ready to leave his home in the mountains and start university in the city. But all that changed for Teff.

Teff, renamed by my own toddler self and still Teff to me now. Teff moving with us into the tiny flat in Bronte before he had a chance to move out and start his own life. Teff changing nappies and walking the floor with a crying baby while our mother waited on tables. Teff, propping up my bottle with his final year economics text books. I made his young life a very serious affair, and he has never, never complained to me about that. I can remember the scream welling out of my child rib-cage "But I never asked to be born!"

Thursday, I'll see Alma. She's the one person I can tell about Bella's presence in her little bedroom. I'll tell her about the scent of lavender and the wet pillow. She won't quiz me about how I know it was Bella who was there. She'll take me through how I am reacting to that, how I am dealing with that, why I can't tell anyone else about that. Bella's secret and mine will be safe with Alma.

I have overstayed my hour in Bella's bedroom. It must be so late. I wander downstairs in the dark, and make myself a cup of tea and a vegemite toast and take it up to my bedroom. I fluff up my pillows and shake out the doona, and get into bed with my tea, toast and my half-read novel. I have to keep going back to the beginning as I forget who is who from one night to the next, and what they are doing, and where they are up to in their book lives. It's no use. I'm not doing so well with these strangers in print tonight either.

I turn off the light and let my thoughts go where they will. Round in circles mostly. I conjure up Bella's face to say good-night to, and God Bless although I wonder how God stayed in our nightly rituals, when He has been banished from my life for some decades now.

I close my eyes and can hear the noises coming from next door's bedroom through the brick wall which separates their house from mine. The tenants, a young couple, have started to make love and I can hear the faint stirrings of her throaty gasps. This is the only noise I ever hear from next door.

The noises of eating, flushing the toilet, talking, singing, playing music never find their way into my house. I wonder if they do any of these daily things.

Perhaps all they do at home is have sex. I start to count the gasping breaths. She usually climaxes in a throaty scream somewhere between the fourteenth and the twenty-sixth breath. I make a mental note, twenty six again. She's lasting longer these days. He makes no sound at all that I can hear.

I see them sometimes, leaving the house at the same time I do in the mornings, or in the evenings, letting themselves into the house, together. Always together. We smile at each other and sometimes exchange a "gooday". That's all. I have no idea who they are, how old they are, how long they have been together, if they are married. There are no smells from their kitchen either. Perhaps they don't eat.

I don't know the people on the other side either. Their house shares the other brick wall which goes the full length of our houses. I see them sometimes, an old woman and her middle aged son. I smile at the old woman, but we don't say anything. I can't smile at the son as he doesn't do eye contact. He hurries in and out of the front door with his eyes firmly fixed on the tops of his shoes, and muttering. There are only two noises which come from their house. One, when the son berates his old mother and calls her stupid for losing things. "You are a human and humans have a brain. Just think where you left it." The other sound is magnificent piano music which he plays long into the night.

I drift off to sleep wondering about all the other people in my street whom I don't even see, or perhaps I do, but don't realise that they are my neighbours. I think back to Sally's grandparents, with the six little children tucked up in their beds on a winter night and the air thick with dust from the black coal fire place. I bet everyone knew everyone else then. I wonder about the cup of sugar they eternally borrowed from each other. What did they need the cup of sugar so urgently for? Or was it some sort of code? Was it some ritual excuse to go into someone else's house for a cup of tea and a gossip? Well there're no cups of teas or sugars now.

The young couple are having a second go now, but she barely reaches 12 gasps. I smile. Serves her right.

4. BELLA

Bella leaves Nick's house early in the morning, before the cleaner gets there. No-one is to know she is staying there. This is only the second time she has left Nick's house since she first arrived, two weeks ago. The first Tuesday she just rode the trains. It was raining, and the railway carriages were at least dry. She first went all the way south to Wollongong, and then back to Sydney, and then got a train to Newcastle, which took forever because it stopped at every station. Then back to Sydney and up to the Blue Mountains. On her school train pass, she could spend the whole day, staring out the window, finding comfort in the changing population of her carriage, and in the movement of the train and in feeling that she was so anonymous that she was almost invisible.

But today was going to be different. She shifts the large shoulder bag she 'borrowed' from Nick's mum to her other side, and walks briskly, feeling so free to be out of Nick's house at last.

It feels wonderful, to be outside in the fresh morning air. It is so lovely, walking to the station, through the broad tree-lined streets, that she almost forgets the enormous mess she has got herself into. She breathes deep the fresh morning air, and marvels yet again, that families actually live in these huge houses in their huge gardens. Compared to her mum's little Paddington terrace, they seem so luxurious, and somehow, so unnecessary. Even her dad's garden unit with lots of open space seems as much as anyone could possibly need.

Nick's house overwhelms her. At first she kept getting lost, forgetting which bathroom she was in. She is more used to it now.

More important, Bella keeps losing the plot. She knows why she ran away. She knows why she went to Nick's. The opportunity was too good to let slip, with his parents overseas and his older brother Chris preferring to hang out with his junkie friends than stay home and look after his sixteen year old little brother.

But, while Bella knew at the time exactly what she was doing, she is not so sure now. Not so sure at all. And her mum! Bella can hardly bear to think about what she is doing to her mum. And her dad. And Uncle Teff. And her step mum Verity. And her friends at school, and her music teacher, and on and on, the list grows in her mind of all the people she loves and is hurting.

Bella has made her way to the station and waits for train to take her into the city.

The train is crowded with commuters, smart men in dark suits, some surprisingly young, with backpacks instead of brief-cases. Most of the women are young and are in black. Black jackets with straight black skirts, black coats draped over an arm, black shoes. Bella looks at them with astonishment. They are all so neat. She cannot imagine that in just a few years time, she and her friends might be working in the city in some business or stockbroking firm, looking so neat. She wonders how you get neat. Or perhaps they were all private school kids who always looked neat in their uniforms. Perhaps they were born that way. Perhaps it comes with living in big spacious houses. With cleaners.

Bella finds a seat, next to the window, so that she can gaze out, and doesn't have to look at the neat commuters. She settles down to a good forty minutes in the train, and lets her mind wander.

She goes back to her big dilemma. Just what is she doing?

It all started, she remembers, when she overheard her dad and his new wife Verity talking in the lounge room. She had wandered into the kitchen to get herself a glass of milk, and was on the way back to bed, but couldn't help stopping when she overheard their conversation.

Her dad was saying very earnestly,

'But are you sure, Verity? Are you absolutely sure? Some of these pregnancy tests can be so unreliable.'

Bella took down a recipe book and pretended to read it. She was caught now. If she made a go for it now, they might see her. If she stayed it looked like she was eavesdropping. Well, she was eavesdropping.

Bella heard Verity explain to Peter that she didn't trust them either, so she had been to the doctor and the examination confirmed it. She was at least eight weeks. Anyway, she went on, she remembered how she had felt when she had Sam and her breasts were already getting bigger and tender to touch.

Verity said it again. 'Hey, Peter, it's OK. I'm pregnant. I am definitely pregnant. It's what we wanted it, wasn't it? Our own child. We have Sam and Bella and now we can have one that is ours.'

And then her father said something that made a chill go up Bella's spine.

'Verity, are you sure I am the father?'

Bella was all attention now. What on earth was her father on about?

Look, I know you and Gina had trouble conceiving Bella. I know you had to go to the fertility clinic and it took ages. But hey, you and me, we're different to you and Gina. This one is totally and completely ours. It worked. It happened. And I'm thrilled.'

'But how can you be so sure that I am the father?'

Verity took a while to answer that one. But her voice was firm and she sounded totally in control of this situation.

'Look Peter, I can understand your doubts. We can get DNA tests if you want. But, honestly Peter, I haven't been with anyone else, I don't want to be with anyone else, I really don't have time to have an affair, and I am perfectly happy with everything the way it is. Relax.'

She went on,

'Peter, the preparation that we have been through for this. You know as well as I do, that things are much better now. Sure, your sperm count was way down years ago, and that's why we went for treatment. It's worked. They said there was a small chance it would and it has. Hey, lighten up. It's what we want. It's what we went for. I want to celebrate.'

Bella heard Peter get up. He must have gone and held her, from the sounds of it, and they did lots of kissing, from the sounds of it. He hadn't even noticed that the kitchen light was still on.

Bella safely tip toed back to her room.

Bella didn't sleep much that night. First, she kept thinking about getting a baby sister or brother. Bella didn't know how she felt about that, except it wasn't all excitement and enthusiasm. She quite liked it the way it was.

It was neat. Verity had her little boy and Peter had his teenage daughter who could stay over as often as she wanted. What was the matter with that?

It was so safe and predictable going to Dad's house. He and Verity both worked, Sam got dropped and picked up from long day care, and meals were on time and highly nutritious. On weekends, there was a routine. Dad got the breakfast, Verity got lunch and dinner and cleaned the kitchen. Dad put on the wash, Verity vacuumed, and they each did one bathroom. Bella was expected to take Sam to the park on a Sunday morning. As they went out the door, she would shout back

'Enjoy the sex'

and slam the door before she could hear the reply

'Bella, please don't talk like that in front of Sam'.

But now things were going to be different.

Bella was really curious about that part of the conversation – the bit about the sperm count and how Verity had been so patient and understanding when Peter had questioned whether he was the father? Were they really saying that Peter had been sterile and was now fertile because the doctors could help with that?

Bella tried to stay with that. First she thought,

'Well if that's the case, it has nothing to do with me,'

But then a little crack appeared, and a little thought squeezed through.

'Did they have to use a donor?

The crack widened and the unwanted thoughts came tumbling through.

'Isn't Peter my real dad?'

'Then they have lied to me, all this time, all my life.'

And finally,

'Well if he is not my father, who is?'

The train stops. Bella looks up to see they are at Town Hall station. She jumps out, runs up the stairs, to another platform, for her train home.

Home.

Bella thinks of the little terrace house she has shared with Gina for almost as long as she can remember. She is hanging out to be in her attic. Her private space. She cannot get there fast enough.

As she gets closer to the house, she puts on Nick's mother's sunnies and hat and scarf that she has 'borrowed'. She doesn't want to be recognised. But then, she thinks, she doesn't really know any of the neighbours, and they don't seem to know her. She reaches into her bag for her tiny bottle of lavender oil and dabs it on her forehead and the back of her neck. This is a ritual that is so comforting for her. She feels safe with the smell of lavender on her body. She has been wearing it ever since she was tiny, when her parents were still together and brought if back from a holiday in Tasmania. Her dad chose it because the pink was her favourite colour. But it was the smell. It tells her that everything is alright.

Bella lets herself into the house. She looks around and is amazed to see it looks exactly the same. Perhaps a little messier. She goes upstairs to her attic room and flops down on the bed. She falls asleep for a while, and wakes up to find that she is crying. She turns the pillow over, remembering when she had bad dreams, Gina would always turn the pillow over. Bella remembered how she used to demand a fresh pillow if she had a second bad dream because she thought both sides of the pillow had bad dreams stuck to them.

She notices the envelope under the pillow and smiles as she tucks it into her bag. She reaches in her pocket for the tiny flower she has picked and places it on top of the pillow.

'Please mum, please smell the lavender. Please know that I have been here and that I am alright.'

She gets up, goes downstairs, out the door, and walks back to the station. She still has three hours to kill before she meets Nick after school. Just this once, they are going on a very special outing.

5. TEFF

I am woken by the telephone invading my dreams. It is only two days since I found the little flower under Bella's pillow, and I reach under my pillow for Bella's note and remind myself I have not been dreaming.

'Hullo', I manage into the phone.

'Hey, little Sis.' It's Teff.

'Happy birthday.'

'Oh Teff. You always remember, don't you.'

'How could I forget. So where am I taking you to dinner tonight?'

'How about Mario's?'

I hear him smiling through the phone. We always go to Mario's. Every year for longer than I care to remember, we go to Mario's on my birthday.

'I'll pick you up at 7.30', he says. 'Bye now.'

'Bye now', I say, but he has gone.

Dear Teff. He is always there for me. I could run to him anytime for help. I could say, "Hey Teff, I need four thousand dollars, or a new car, or a good cry." And he would be there for me. But I don't. I hardly ever call him. Sometimes I even forget about him. Yet he is my only bit of family that is left.

I lie back in bed for a luxurious stretch, another ten minutes, another thirty if I skip breakfast.

Teff saved my mother's life. It if were not for him growing inside her, she would never have fled Germany. They had such a bond with their shared escape. Then together and alone in this strange land.

I have never really got over my jealousy of Teff, that he had our mother while she was young and vibrant. Because he had her laughter and her fun and her games. I don't wish he hadn't had those things. I just wish that I had had them too.

And then Teff had even more. The beautiful golden haired child charmed his way into his new Italian family. With his blue eyes like saucers, his continual chatter and babble, he turned our mother's employees into aunties and uncles, papa and mama. They doted on him, teaching him Italian, teaching him how to croon arias, to show off his muscles, to eat pasta with a big white serviette tucked into his shirt and to embrace life as a precious gift from the blessed Maria herself.

Yes. I do feel cheated. I want to shout out, 'Hey, they are my family. I'm the one who is half Italian here! Why don't I know them? Why didn't they shower their love on me?'

Oh this is a pathetically dark and victim space I am slipping into on my birthday.

Stop it!

OK. Let's try this. Mostly I am glad he had such a charmed childhood. It must have been so hard for him later, playing father to me while all his friends were out having fun. Poor Teff, trying to support our mother who just worked and worked and worked, working off her sin and Rosa's death.

Now Teff is still a very serious person. He is a very serious stockbroker. He makes a serious lot of money. He is a serious father and such a serious husband that I marvel that his relationship stays intact while everyone else's falls apart. And he is still a very serious big brother. He never forgets my birthday. I shudder. I am forty-nine. When she was forty-nine I was ten. No I am not going there today. No way.

Then how old is Teff? He must be sixty-eight! But that is so old. He doesn't look sixty-eight or whatever you are supposed to look like then. He doesn't even have grandchildren. But his children. I wonder if he still sees them every Friday night for Sabbath dinner. They might be all grown up and independent, but I bet he knows exactly where they are at all times. I shudder.

I look at the clock. Shit. I'll be late again. I jump out of bed and throw on yesterday's clothes. I will shout myself breakfast at an Italian cafe on the way to work. Happy birthday to me.

We are sitting at Mario's after a memorable meal, Teff and I. Teff has broken everyone of his skinny wife's diet rules and his arteries must be fairly giggling with bubbles of saturated fats. I am feeling a glow that comes with very expensive and old Italian red wine. Every part of my physical body feels deliciously content.

Teff is very good at keeping the conversation rolling. He is so effortlessly the big brother and I account to him on all aspects of my life. Between mouthfuls I am audited. My job, on the performance indicators of how secure it is, how well I am being paid, how satisfying it is, prospects for promotional positions and, of course, how much is going into my super fund.

Then my house. No, I have not had to take out any more loans. Yes, I do still enjoy living there. No, there are no major repairs needed at the moment. Redecorating? I laugh. Teff, that word is just not in my vocabulary. I feel relieved as the essential business side of my life has been revealed and seems to have passed the Teff test.

As always Teff does not pry into my love life but most of all I am relieved that he does not mention Bella. He just squeezes my hand and says he knows that things must be really hard for me at the moment and could he suggest that he could pay for a very good private detective ..... Thanks, but no thanks, Teff. No, really. He has friends. He has contacts with the police. He knows people who may know people who know how you go about this on different levels. I smile up at him through huge tears that run shamelessly down my cheeks, and manage a "No, not yet, but thanks, Teff, thanks.'

Teff asks about the calls to Bella from the public phone boxes. I tell him the police found the addresses for me and I drove around and found all four. But their positions meant nothing to me. Nor to the police.

'I've been thinking about Mama' I say, "since Bella ran off.'

I cannot say ''ran away'. I cannot put into words that she has run away from me, from our home together, from our life together.

'I'm glad Mama is not here to know about this. I would feel so ashamed, I don't think I could face her.'

Teff just sits and looks at me patiently.

'I always felt that I had let her down anyway. I was never good enough for her, for her high expectations of me. I know I was nothing like what she wanted her daughter to be. Strong and decisive and independent, like she was.'

'A survivor,' he says.

'A survivor', I agree.

'Yes. I see them all the time, little Sis. In my work, in the community. New disasters and wars bring new survivors here. Survivors – ones who flee the oppressive governments, escaped the coups, the wars and the ethnic cleansing.'

Teff went silent.

'Go on,' I prompt.

'I often wonder about these survivors and their children. The ones I see. So many of them want to talk to me about their disappointments in their children. These children, now growing up, don't seem to be the same strong and tough survivors or perhaps they are survivors in a different way. Perhaps life for them is a different struggle, and their parents just can't see it.'

I know what Teff is saying. I conjure up the people I know, the ones like the ones Teff is talking about, ones like us, Teff and me. I blurt out 'Perhaps it's really hard, having parents who are survivors.'

'Perhaps.' He shrugged. 'Perhaps they think they have been through so much and that they have protected their children from serious harm and so their children should be able to breeze through life. To take the good with none of the bad. Not really bad. Not bad like they had. Hardly bad at all. But their children don't breeze through life. And the parents tell their stockbroker. They tell me that they cannot understand their children. They tell me because I sit there and listen. I do not contradict them. So they just keep talking. What am I supposed to do with all of that?'

Poor Teff. What indeed?

Pathetically I offer.

'Well you can always tell me.'

But confusions of my own are beginning to surface.

'But Teff. I always thought it was different with you and Mama. I thought you were everything she wanted. I thought it was only me she was so disappointed in.'

'Ah, Caro,' he sighed, finding my pet name from so long ago, 'you hang on to my perfect childhood. Sure, she was younger and more alive. But, she was always Bella first, and Mama second. And that is the sad, sad truth for both of us.'

He went on, 'We're wounded, both of us. We aren't losers, as the kids would say now. But we never come first either. Perhaps we are seconds. We reach for good enough, never best. We never feel, deep down, that we deserve to be the best. By her standards, we did no real suffering or loss. By her standards, we couldn't compete. And the damn stupid part of it was that suffering and loss was what she was trying to protect us from, and in doing so, she handed it out. Big time.'

I look at Teff and I feel incredibly sad, like we are two abandoned children, clinging onto the tatters of our childhoods.

He reaches over and covers my clenched hands with his large fingers.

'Caro, you have nothing, nothing to be ashamed of with this Bella thing. Our Mama was not half the parent you are. You have made a child with spirit. You have given that spirit room to live and grow. Bella is out there testing her limits – how far she can go with something she has to do. When she has done this, she will come home. I know that and so do you, don't you?'

'Yes' I whisper.'

'Can't hear you.'

'Yes' I say louder.

'Yes. Yes. Yes. Teff, I know she is safe. Teff, I know it, I know it. I know it.'

Blessedly, he does not ask how I know. I am not ready to tell even Teff that. I have a deep fear that if I talk about it, it will shatter. Her visits will stop. I will have broken some pact I was never party to in the first place.

I reach for some lightness for my birthday dinner.

'What is your happiest memory, of when you were little, eh Teff?'

He thinks for a long while, as the waiter places the coffees before us, and pushes his chair a little away from the table. He looks at a space above my head, and talks to it.

'It was my time with Pluto. We got him when he was a tiny puppy and I was allowed to name him after the only dog I knew and that was from the comic books. So he was Pluto and he became my closest friend. Only he wasn't allowed to sleep on my bed. Every night, even in the coldest part of winter, he was sent outside to his big kennel where I was allowed to give him a hot water bottle wrapped in a blanket. But where do you think he slept?'

I shake my head and shrug. This is the first I've ever heard of Pluto.

'On the flat roof of the kennel. Even when he grew too big, he would curl up so that he could fit on top. After a while, Alfredo felt so sorry for him he moved the kennel onto the verandah, but he still slept on the roof. Pluto was such a good listener. I told him all my secrets.'

'What happened to him?'

'He lived out his life with lots of love and attention. And then he grew old and died. That's not too bad, is it? But at the time, of course I was really sad. I felt I had lost a brother.'

I shake off the images of the life of Pluto and put a question which I ask him every birthday dinner.

"And you, Teff. How is it with you?"

I expect the usual "Fine" which kills off any further enquiry. Instead, he gets up, scraping his chair on the terra cotta tiles.

'Let's take a walk', he says.

As he pays the bill I am in awe of the long row of plastic cards in his wallet and amazed at how his fingers seek out the one to pay for this meal as, at the same time, his brain seeks out the exact amount of money to add for the tip. We walk outside into a perfect Bondi spring evening. We head in the direction of the slight breeze blowing in from the ocean, and, still in silence, we fall into step with each other.

This is very strange for me. I can feel a struggle going on inside Teff, my big protector brother. I want to wait for him to start talking in his own time. But of course I don't.

'What is it Teff?' I say. 'Talk to me.'

He reaches down and links his arm to mine. His free arm starts waving about as he emphasises the points he cannot make.

Then he starts.

'Gina', he starts. 'Do you realise I am heading towards seventy?'

'I find myself looking back on it all, and it doesn't shape up, Gina. It isn't the life I thought I would have. It has all the trimmings and not much of the essentials. Or perhaps it has all the essentials and the trimmings are missing.'

'Mmm.'

'It feels disloyal to Mirium', he goes on, 'to talk to you about all this, but, you're family, Gina. You're all the old family I've got, you know.'

Yes, I did know.

'I've often wondered about my father. My real father. Especially lately. I usen't to. It wasn't important to me when I was growing up, or even when my children were growing up. But it does now. I feel that I have had my family, and the big Vincento family, and you and Mum family, but never him.'

I felt pangs about never really seeing my real father too. About Alfredo not wanting to know me when Teff used to take me up the mountains for a visit. We had a lot in common, me and Teff. I made an effort to shut out my stuff and concentrate on his, just for tonight. I made myself feel open to whatever it was he wanted to tell me.

'Even though I couldn't have been more than two when we left, I can still remember the first family our mother worked for when she arrived here. The Golds. In Rose Bay. My earliest memories are the big Friday night shabasses in the dining room, with candles, the men with their yarmulkehs on their head. I can still remember the house. The big kids would play with me. Johnathon would give me rides on his shoulders and Sarah would push me to the shops in the pram, and put ribbons in my hair and pretend to the shopkeepers that I was her little sister.

'Have you ever seen them, since then?

'No. Mum never talked about why we left. I can remember asking her later. But she would just change the subject. You know, how she could do that. When I first came down to Sydney I had friends who lived quite close to that house. Often, when I was staying with them, I would get up early in the morning and walk past the Gold's place and hang about waiting to see if any of them lived there any more. It seemed so long ago. Even then. Even then when I was a student.

Once a middle-aged man I didn't recognise came out in his dressing-gown to get the morning paper. I felt like I was snooping. I guess I was. I suppose I could really find them if I really wanted to, probably just Johnathon and Sarah now. But there doesn't seem much point. They were very kind people, the Golds. But they weren't like family.'

My picture of the nineteen forties wealthy Jewish family around the Friday night table, seen through the golden vaseline lens faded as I waited for Teff to close down on this reverie and get to wherever he was heading.

'If I ever thought that was a family, honestly Gina, it was nothing compared to life at the Roma Guest House.'

I looked up at my big brother. I had felt his step lighten. His face was almost glowing under the old-fashioned lamps on the beach front.

'Gina, this was some family we moved into. It was so ..... It was so ...... It was so alive. Oh, Gina, if only you had been there. The kitchen was my favourite place.

Papa and Mama and great aunty Nina, and aunts and uncles and cousins, friends and even friends with more friends. Our Mama was so beautiful then, Gina. She was so loved. By all of them. They would sing her name, Bella, Bella, Bella, Bellaaaaa. And she would sing back. German songs. Italian songs. Opera songs. And the same guest house families would come back for their holidays year after year, and they would become part of the big family and come into the kitchen. And then there were times, like in mid-winter, when no one would come and Papa would close down the heating so that the only warm room was the kitchen, and we would spend all of our time there. At bedtime, Mama and I would race up the freezing cold stairs and jump into our beds, piling on all the doonas we could find. Mama and I would laugh when we had so much bedding we couldn't roll over in bed.'

'Gina.' He sobered up suddenly.

'Gina. Where has it all gone. Mirium and I, we didn't do those crazy thing. We didn't laugh with the children till we nearly wet our pants. We didn't break into songs at the dinner table. We didn't squash just one more and just one more around the table until we were so close we had to take it in turns to lean forward and fork pasta into our mouths. My children did not hide their grandparent's glasses letting them think that they had forgotten where they had put them again. They didn't even have real grandparents, or a crazy old great aunt, or unexpected guests.'

His mouth stopped talking, and, as if connected by strings, his feet stopped walking and his hand stopped in an outstretched gesture of despair. He turned to face me and spun me by my shoulders to face him holding onto my shoulders very tightly.

'Gina. My family life is so boring. My wife is boring. I am boring. My children are boring. We are all successful and boring. And Gina. Sometimes I don't think I can stand one more night in my perfectly decorated house, with its colour co-ordinated bedroom, and its squeaky clean en suite with my perfect Zegna suits lined up in my perfect dressing-room. But of course, I will.'

"What do you want, Teff?'

'I want to feel free and young before I get too old. I want my wife to feel free and my kids, too.'

'Me too, Teff. I want to feel free too. I want to be free of grief and guilt.'

'Little Sis. When this is over for you, and I have a feeling that she will come back, let's you and I go find our roots. How about I take you to Berlin and we find out where we're really from.'

He lets go of my shoulders and I shrug them back into place. 'Yes. Let's.'

We walk back in silence broken by Teff as he tells me of his recurrent dream. He can call up that dream when he goes for walks at night. It kicks in with the rhythm of his black lace-up leather shoes striking the footpath on his nightly walk.

I remind myself that Teff has had many obsessions over the years, although we have never really spoken about them. I am acutely away that he is about to share one with me now.

I watch him walking. I can hear his shoes making clipped sounds on the pavement, tat, tat, tat, and I can hear his voice echo the same rhythm, tat, tat, tat as we walk slowly along the beach promenade.

Each night after dinner, he tells me, he asks his wife Mirium if she would like to go for a walk with him, and each night she says, "No thank you, dear" and each night he is glad because he can relive this nightmare which visits him. Sometimes he allows himself the possibility that if Mirium did come with him for his walk, he would not be able to relive the nightmare and it may go away for good. But he does not want it to go away for good. He doesn't know why. Why doesn't really matter.

As he summons up the dream, he tells me he is back in school, but not his school. The headmaster is there with a heavy tread and a cane that goes swoosh, swoosh, swoosh as he swings it by his side. This headmaster is not from Teff's school days. He speaks German. Teff answers in English.

'How many trains?'

'Fifteen every day.'

'How many carriages?'

'23.'

'Who goes to the left?'

'The old and the children.'

'Who goes to the right?'

'The young men and women.'

'How many huts?'

'19'

'How many per hut?'

'750'

'So, Stefan, how many people are in the camp?' Swoosh.

Stefan panics. He does not have enough information and he has too much information. He needs to sort it out. What does he really need? Does the headmaster mean how many people come into Birkenau? He tries to work it out in his head. Do trains run every day? Every 365 day of the year? How many years? But how can I multiply that by 15 trains, and how many people fit into each of the 23 carriages? And how many die each day? He hasn't been told that. Or does he just have to concentrate on the numbers of cabins? Is it just 19 by 750? He can do that in his head. Just do it by 20 and subtract 750. But that is only if the camp is full. Nobody has told him how many children and old people there were compared to the healthy young adults.

'Well Stefan?' Swoosh.

He tries to reason with the headmaster. He becomes Stefan the grown man who has some standing in the community. He gives to charities. He has his own stock-broking company. His wife is a lawyer. He has grown up children himself. He is no longer a child he'll have you know.

The headmaster screams at him in German.

'How many?' Swoosh.

Teff knows that first he has to stop walking. Then he has to re-focus his eyes on something, anything, a bush, a lamp-post, a dog. But he always leaves it to the last possible moment. He has to hold out as long as he possibly can. He waits and he waits until the long thin cane is raised over the headmaster's shoulder. He waits till it starts its downward rush. He waits until it is inches from his outstretched hands.

One day, he knows, he will wait too long.

Teff stops walking. He stops recanting the waking, walking dream. He takes a deep breath and a shudder moves through his body. He tells me that he has done many variations of this dream in many camps. He has calculated the train schedules. He has calculated the number of man-work-days. He has done the catering sums, if you could call that catering. He has done audits on the piles of spectacles, suitcases and teeth. He has brokered all kinds of death stock.

I feel that I am a chosen recipient of this madness and I can sense his relief that one other human being knows what goes on in his head.

'The holocaust,' he says, 'is in my DNA. It is embedded in my cells. It's why we still have to write books about it, make movies about it. It will take generations to wash out and then it will be gone.'

For once I have nothing to say.

We reach the car. We drive home in silence.

He pulls up in front of my little terrace house and he leans across to give me a kiss. We tell each other we love each other. At this moment, I feel that we are all we have.

6. NICK

Nick is sixteen, the same age as Bella. In fact they share the same star sign. They are both Aries. They share a secret. They both don't know who their real fathers are. They call their unknown fathers "the wankers". All they know about their fathers is that they wanked into test-tubes for the sperm bank – seventeen years ago.

Nick and Bella have taken time out of their lives to prepare and carry out a very important job. Nick has been planning it for a long time.

Fate has been kind to them and given them a helping hand by way of getting Nick's family out of the picture. Nick's parents have gone overseas for seven weeks. They have left Nick in the care of his older brother Chris. They have done this before, with shorter trips, and it has worked out. But now Chris has developed a heroin habit. He is hardly ever home. He manages to pretend that he is looking after things at home. He calls his parents on their mobile every week and tells them that everything is fine. Sometimes he calls Nick, and offers to drop by, but Nick tells him everything is fine. Chris teases Nick that he has a chick staying. Nick plays along. After all, it's true.

Nick is managing to keep it together too. He buys in the food, pays the weekly cleaner, does the lawns, waters the gardens, feeds the dog, gets himself to school and keeps Bella hidden from the neighbours and the cleaner who comes in on Tuesdays. Nick is very competent.

It is very comfortable at Nick's house. There are five bedrooms, three with their own bathrooms, two television sets with built in video and DVD players, a big spa bath and a pool. But Nick takes care that Bella is not seen in the garden, except on the odd weekend, as if she might be visiting Nick. Nick takes care that no other friends visit him, especially when Bella leaves her things out. But on the whole Bella does not have things.

Bella doesn't go to school anymore. She works on the plan and on keeping out of sight. Nick sets her work to do on the internet every day. He also brings home the work they have done at school so that she doesn't get too far behind. Nick and Bella are both trying to be very responsible about the whole thing.

Bella is still seduced by the whole idea of blowing up the sperm bank. It is simple. It is final. It makes a big statement that they, the sperm bank children, do not like the way they were conceived, and that the adults who are supposed to be responsible, have stuffed up, again. She thinks Nick is very clever and very brave to have thought it up. In a way, it is fun. And it is actually doing something instead of just talking about it. There is so much Bella knows she can do nothing about. She can do nothing about stopping wars, killings, wiping out species or overpopulation of the human species. She wants to make a difference. She wants to change so much. Meanwhile here's Nick working out how to make a difference. How to make them see kids, no matter how they were conceived, want a father who is more than sperm in a test-tube. That kids like us are angry. Like we didn't ask to get conceived that way. We can sure let them know that we don't approve. Big time.

Bella is becoming an expert on all aspects of IVF and especially sperm banks. She has found out that the sperm is stored in huge stainless steel freezers set at minus 77 degrees. She and Nick were disappointed to learn that in Sydney there are several sperm banks because they really wanted there to be only one. But they know which one is the biggest. It's in one of the largest hospitals in western Sydney. And you can walk past it, on the way to the maternity wards. They know. They went there last Tuesday after Nick had finished school, to suss it out.

Bella has also found out that, for children their age, there are no records linking sperm from the sperm bank with the names of their donors who were mostly medical students. As sperm bank children Nick and Bella have no way of finding out who their real fathers are. They may have the same father, for all they know.

Sometimes Bella takes time off from her research to imagine him. She draws him. She fantasises about meeting him.

Bella is grateful that her parents needed sperm rather than eggs as eggs were so much harder to come by seventeen years ago. But she finds out, that now, in the USA, you can buy eggs on websites like Creating Families Inc. and if you have $10,000 to spend you can choose from a catalogue. The women who are most in demand are those who can produce up to 60 eggs at a time. It takes ten days of injecting a hormone mix into the fat of her lower belly, lots of ultrasounds to check on the egg production, and a general anaesthetic to put her to sleep while they gently pump out the little eggs. But, bingo, if you are blond, have blue eyes and a high IQ you can pay off your credit card debt with one order from a wealthy eggless couple. Well, that is what the advertisements say. Bella also finds out that she can play mix and match with the sperm catalogue. The sperm too come with the best qualities. They are from big strong young men, in immaculate health with sparkling eyes and smooth skin. She searches her reflection in the mirror, but she doesn't seem to find anyone there remotely resembling the guys in the catalogue.

Nick researches explosives and the rights of IVF children. He has discovered the site of Tangled Web Inc. and has put his favourite quote as a screen saver, so that Bella sees it every single time she turns on his computer. It says, 'It is essential to switch the focus of Donor Conception from meeting the needs of adults to defending the rights of people born as a result and protecting them from the intrinsic injustices of the practice.'

Nick reads that British fertility clinics are now required to register the donors in a data base that the offspring can look at when they are eighteen years old. He has also found out that the boss of one of the biggest USA fertility clinics was quoted as saying that it would devastate the industry if they brought that in.

Nick wonders just who that would be devastating to. Like perhaps to the doctor who ran one fertility clinic and inseminated seventy-five patients with his own sperm. Nick can get very angry about stories like that. Like, did the mums know each other? Did they recognise that their little darlings all looked a bit alike, and reminded them a bit of, now who could that be?

Nick is beginning to feel the strain. It is harder on him, as he often reminds Bella. He's the one who has to do most of the covering. He is the only one who is still going to school. He joins in conversations at school which take place with endless speculation as to what could have happened to Bella. He listens to everyone else's theory about her, and puts in a few of his own. He suggests that she has joined a travelling rock band. Nick has to be careful when he does the shopping as he also tells Bella. Not too much food from one supermarket. Not too much at the same chemist's. Not too much so that it eats into his spending budget. Bella tries not to eat too much. But she is so bored at home everyday by herself. She can't help feeling nibbly.

Nick has to be careful at home. He is the only one to answer the door. Answer the phone. Always expect the unexpected, he tells her. Bella has stopped expecting anything at all. After all, it is the same, day after day. Except Tuesdays.

Nick doesn't like being reminded that it is also hard on Bella. But it is. The initial excitement has worn off and sometimes this whole thing feels like a really stupid mistake. The strain of being locked up in the house is beginning to tell on her too but she knows she must keep it together for Nick. Sometimes he looks so vulnerable. He has started to get dark circles under his eyes. He stays up late at night and Bella thinks that he must be on speed to keep him going. So Bella pretends to be in control. She sooths Nick with what he wants to hear. She always has the sort of information he wants to see, as soon as he comes home from school.

And she tries so hard not to question him about her friends at school. She knows that he doesn't pay any attention at all to the things that matter so much to her. He doesn't notice who is hanging around with who, who is having lunch together, who is playing music with who, who is having sleepovers. But she wants to know. And he is there every day while she stays at his place and does all the things he writes down for her to do. She would give anything to go to school, just for one day. But that is against the rules. No school. No going home. No phone calls. No emails. No letters.

Most nights they watch a few TV programs together. They don't drink. They don't smoke dope. Nick gets very prickly at the suggestion. He says he doesn't want to end up like his brother Chris.

'I'm strong' he told Bella. 'And I care what I put in my body. I'm not going to fuck with my mind. No way.'

Bella is so glad that Nick doesn't know that she has been going home.

'What did you do all day?' he asks, the minute she comes in the front door, this Tuesday, and last Tuesday and the one before.

'Just travelled the trains, and walked in the botanical gardens. Next week I might go to a movie.'

'As long as no-one sees you. You didn't see anyone you know?'

'No'

'You didn't catch the train at end of school time?'

'No'

'You didn't ...'

'No Nick. No. No. No. I didn't do anything.'

'Well I wish you wouldn't smell so much of that pink oil stuff. It stinks'

Bella knows that she can, in fact, go home whenever she likes. This is what saves her. She is not a prisoner in this house. She wonders why she feels like one.

Bella thinks about this a lot lately. And as much as she does not want to think about it, she has started to think about what keeps her there and she knows it is also tied up with what is happening to Nick. At first she was there because it seemed such a good idea but now she knows she is there because some-one has to keep a watch on Nick. This thought is terrifying.

Nick is getting jumpier. His voice sounds just that bit shriller when he talks to his parents on the phone. He goes totally out of control on Monday nights, stuffing Bella's few things in hiding places, putting away cups, glasses, plates, anything that might look like someone else is staying. He airs the bathroom and complains again about her lavender smell. He even asks if she is having a period and what she has done with her tampons. He scrubs the spar tub yelling out that the cleaner knows he doesn't use the bloody thing. Sometimes he phones his brother Chris and asks him to come over on Tuesday mornings. Chris doesn't.

Now Nick has started yelling at Bella that they are slowing down. They are not getting through the plan. They are behind. She should be looking for more explosive sites for him to look up. Not just how to make them, but where you can buy the stuff. What exactly you need. How much. They should have all of that information by now. Look at the plan. Look. Week four and they are hopelessly not there.

Nick is suddenly scared of leaving trails. How will he buy what he needs? Over the net? That will leave a trail. He can't use the credit card his father left for him. Can he get a false credit card? Can she find out? Tomorrow? Can she put it on her list? Well of course he doesn't know or otherwise he wouldn't be asking her to find out, would he? Would he? Would he? Bella doesn't like it when Nick goes red in the face and repeating the same question, closes in on her personal space so that she can feel his hot breath as he screams into her face.

Nick is feeling like he is carrying the whole show. And it has always been that way. Ever since he can remember. And, for Nick, the terrible thing is that no-one else in the family realised that, in his own childish way, he was keeping the family together.

Lately Nick has been wondering why his parents went to so much trouble to have children. After all, they both had busy lives running a big time advertising company. Nick's dad looked after all the overseas clients, and was always running off to the States or Europe to meet with the directors of the big companies. Nick's mum was meant to keep the Sydney office running smoothly.

Nick can remember the wonderful times when his dad came home. There were always presents – the latest video games and books. But most of all there was Dad. Dad would take him and Chris surfing and bush walking and to football matches. Dad would take them anywhere for dinner, even McDonalds. Dad would tell them stories of growing up on a sheep farm and how the kids were allowed to ride the old motor bike when their age got to double numbers.

Even Mum was better when Dad was around. She got up more often. She put on pretty clothes and make-up so that her eyes looked big and round.

Sometimes Nick's dad would talk about their mum.

'She wasn't always like this, you know', he would say.

'She used to be so full of life. Then, things started to go wrong – a bit wrong, when you were a baby Chris, and then a bit more after you were born, Nick.'

And sometimes Chris and Dad would talk about how Chris did remember the good times with Mum, and the fun games she would make up.

But then, Chris also remembered a lot more than Nick did, of the really bad times, when Nick was very small and when she would get drunk and didn't seem to know what she was doing at all. Or she was depressed and just not there for any of them.

Most of all Nick remembered her closed bedroom door.

Sometimes he would knock softly wanting to go in for even a short little while, to tell her something important, or perhaps to feel her hand stroking his hair. But mostly he heard a 'not now Nick, perhaps later.'

And for Nick, the terrible thing was, that he never knew if she was going to call out for him to come and lie next to her and tell her what he had been doing all day, or if he was going to be sent away, again.

Nick knew that he had to be good. If Nick was good, then he could keep the family together. If he was good, his dad eventually came home from his trips. If he was good, his mum did come out of her bedroom, get dressed up and throw herself into being a success. If he was very good, then he would not be sent to boarding school, like Chris. Because, Chris, he knew, was not good. Everyone talked about the naughty things Chris had done. Chris, Nick knew, deserved to go to boarding school. But, without him, in the house, he was so lonely.

Nick was often told that he was very bright. The best present he ever got was when his Dad gave him his own computer. Everyone was amazed how quickly he got the hang of it. Everyone had no idea of the games he downloaded. Suddenly little Nick was in charge. He could kill. He could explode. He could blow up planets in outer space we hadn't even heard of.

Now Nick stopped knocking on his mother's closed bedroom door. Who wanted to lie in that smelly room anyway? He no longer had any intention of telling her what he had been doing all day.

And now there were only three weeks to go to complete the plan. They were past half time but there was still so much to do. Nick was having second thoughts about Bella. Why couldn't she take a few initiatives herself? Why did he have to think it all up? Why wouldn't she pay attention in the planning sessions? They still needed to work out how much weight they would have to carry and how easily they could get it all on and off trains. They still needed to work out how to get the stuff into the hospital? What sort of bags? What time of day would be best? Or night? Or would they go in by day and hide till night?

Yes, that would be better. And then? After they lit the fuse? Which way would they run? They needed to time themselves running the length of the corridors, so that they knew how long it would take to escape. The last thing they wanted was to blow themselves up.

The more Nick thought about it, the more there was to think about it. After school, after he had done his homework, after he had put in research on the computer and worked on the plan, after a few tabs to keep him going a bit longer, Nick would eventually go to bed, his heart pounding in the pillow. He lay on his back so that he would not hear the beating in his ears so loudly. He was hot, and he tossed, and just as the first bloody kookaburras started their revolting noise, he fell asleep for a few hours before it was time to get up and start the whole thing again. Once more he was holding it together. Hang in there, he kept telling himself. We are doing it for all those hundreds of thousands of kids, who have been designer babies to all those stupid half sterile couples.

7. VERITY

It is Friday afternoon at work, and I get a phone call from Verity, Peter's wife.

'Verity?' I say, with the rising inflections of a teenager. For a moment I forget who she is. My body has gone back into it's brown school uniform with the box pleats and my head is declining Latin 'Verito veritas, veritat ...'

'Oh, hi Verity!' And now I sound too enthusiastic, like I've been waiting to hear from this person all week. And that's not how I want to sound at all.

She pretends not to notice. But then, she doesn't really know me and perhaps she thinks I'm like this all the time. She says she has been summoning up courage to phone me for a few days. She says she didn't want to phone me at work, but she noticed I didn't pick up the phone at home much. She wonders if I'd mind awfully if she came over, or perhaps we could meet somewhere else if I'd rather.

I do a quick calculation. I leave early on Thursdays for my session with Alma, but I don't want to tell Verity that, so I lie that I will be tied up at work till sixish and how about she comes around about seven, and we can have a drink.

She says that will be fine.

I am stunned. I am curious. I see her as the beautiful new wife of my ex, Peter. We have little chats when I drop Bella around or pick her up after her weekend visit.

I sense that Verity has a cold space around her which I do not want to enter. Yet I entrust my precious Bella to her care, because Peter is her father, and Verity is his wife.

But first there is my precious time with Alma, so I grab my bag, wave a good bye to my work mates who don't seem to notice, and fly out of the tower block building.

Alma has been my safety valve over these last few weeks. She has been the only one I have dared tell my worst scenarios to. I wonder what she does with all this shit. By the end of the day she must have got layers and layers of the stuff dumped on her, like shrouds.

But she calls 'Come in' as I push open her unlocked front door, and gives me a smile and a 'Hello Gina, nice to see you', as if she has just got out of the shower. Perhaps she does shower between every client. I would.

I have been thinking, in the car, on the way to Alma's how I want to explore with her, how the balance between Teff and I has been subtly changing so I haven't even noticed till last night that we are more like equal adults now, both with raw scars and unfulfilled needs, but then I realise that this can all wait, and isn't all that important really, and I burst straight in with 'She's alright. I know she is alive and I think she is alright.'

And instead of exploring the possibilities and probabilities that it is Bella who took the money and left the tiny clover flower, and the whys and hows she is living the way she is at the moment, we go straight into gratitude for small certainties, and coping with big uncertainties, and on the huge spectrum of coping and not coping I can feel myself inching to the coping flagpole barely visible at the end of the long sandy beach. And by the time my fifty minutes is up, there is a smaller than usual pile of screwed up soggy tissues in the bowl beside me, and I feel like I am really doing OK.

On the way out, Alma casually asks if I have talked to Peter about the latest developments. I don't need to say the 'no' word. She just as casually asks if I might think about doing that. Mmmmm.

I drive away, knowing that I will make it through the weekend and that on Monday I will scurry back to the diversion that work has become and that Monday night I can go walking with Terry and that on Tuesday, there will be another sign and that somewhere in between I need to see Peter.

But, I remembered, for now, there is Verity.

I race home. I tell myself that there is no need to tidy up the house, and as I walk around, putting away the pile of newspapers, tossing out the dead flowers and fluffing up the cushions on the blue velvet lounge, I wonder if she was concerned when Peter was coming over every night after dinner. I wonder if she is concerned that he doesn't do that anymore. I wonder if she is beginning to have problems with Peter. I wonder if she wants to talk to someone who has also lived with his moodiness, his days of silence, his big long downers which can last for weeks and weeks, his black depression which seeps out of his body and oozes into every corner of the house. I'm not sure I want to talk with her about Peter. It suits me much better to have Peter happily married. It stops me feeling guilty about not having been able to have made it through the sickness and health bit. It feels good to have at least one person in my life who is OK and it might as well be Peter.

But it wouldn't be Peter she wants to talk about. She'd have women friends she could talk to much more easily about that. She doesn't need me. Anyway, it would be different with her and Peter, different to what it was like for us. I put on the kettle and absent-mindedly lay out some chocolate biscuits, dismissing the notion that seven o'clock at night is a ridiculous time for Tim-Tams. Anyway, I could certainly do with some Tim-Tams, and I get a few down before the front door bell rings.

I shout my totally unnecessary and habitual 'Coming', open the door and there she is, the beautiful young Verity, neat bodied, well made up, hair cut so chic, and composed.

She follows my suggestion that she sit, while I fill up the tray with coffee plunger, mugs, milk, sugar and the plate of chocolate biscuits. I notice she sits straight, perched on the edge of the sofa, her ankles neatly crossed, her hands relaxed in her lap. I feel large, lumpy, untidy and old. I also feel nervous. I tell her that I am pleased that she has made contact, but that I am feeling rather anxious and could we please start off by her telling me why she wanted to see me. And does she take milk and sugar? Of course not.

'It's about Bella.'

I'm all ears. My skin prickles like I'm a stalking animal. I am suspended in time and space until the next words come out of her pretty little mouth.

'Gina, I don't know where she is and I haven't heard from her or seen her.'

'Oh.'

'But there was something. It was a few weeks before she went missing, when she was over at our place, and, I seemed to have put it out of my mind but lately, it keeps coming back to me.'

Verity is softening before my eyes. Her edges have got less sharp. She really has lovely eyes. And they look straight at me.

'I don't really know if it is important, but let me just tell you about it.'

I nod.

She tells me that she thinks Bella might have overheard a conversation she and Peter were having. They were in the lounge room and they thought Bella had gone to bed, but

Verity thought she heard something in the kitchen and looking back she thought Bella might have overheard them.

She was telling Peter that she was pregnant. She had to convince him that it was his child and that the fertility treatment had worked for him. She had to show him it was something to be happy about and that he was going to be a real father for this first time. This child was his in every sense.

Verity said that Peter responded very badly at first and thought she must have been having an affair. She said it took some time to talk him around.

Verity said that she didn't think anything of it at the time, but later she remembered that in the morning the kitchen light was still on, and perhaps Bella had been in the kitchen while they were talking. She said she couldn't be sure, but she knew that Bella wasn't her usual self for the rest of the weekend.

Verity stopped. She was looking very uncomfortable about this whole event.

'Gina, I tried to get Peter to talk to her, to tell her about the pregnancy and to ask her if there was anything about this that upset her in any way. But he shrugged me off. She said he would do it later. He said he wanted to get used to the idea himself.'

'So, Gina, I ended up telling her myself. She wasn't too impressed, but didn't seem to want to talk about it. So I let it go.'

'But then', Verity went on, 'a few nights later, Peter just let it slip that Bella didn't know she was a sperm donor baby and he didn't want to talk about that either.'

'That's when I got really mad at him and told him he had to talk to Bella and somehow explain why she had never been told the truth. He said he would, sometime soon.'

My heart went out to Verity. You have a much wanted planned pregnancy and you end up with a sulky teenager and a sulky partner.

Verity bent forward and took my hands in hers.

'Gina,' she said, 'I had no idea. And I wasn't making the right connections. But then the penny dropped. If Bella had overheard us, then she would have heard for the first time, that Peter was not her biological father and his talk with her about this somehow hasn't happened.'

Well, yes, I could really relate to somehow that didn't happen.

The thoughts came tumbling through my mind. I remembered how Peter could never quite forgive me for being fertile while his low sperm count meant that we tried and tried and tried to have a child for years while all around us couples were having one, two, three perfect children without even trying. I remembered how Peter agreed that we would use a sperm donor on the condition that his child would never know it wasn't his sperm. The same Peter who appears on our daughter's birth certificate as her father and who was and indeed is her father in every way other than biological.

I look at Verity in amazement. Could her beauty crank up his sperm count in his mid forties where I had failed to raise the critical mass in his twenties? How about all the misshapen little ones that we were told about? How about the double whammy that the count was low and most of them would have trouble doing the sperm marathon up my tubes?

Verity must have sensed my feelings. She told me that things had improved in the treatment of male infertility and that there were ways now of concentrating the sperm count to increase the chances of conceiving. But more to the point, she said that she was so sorry that Bella might have found out about all of this and no-one was talking to her about it.

Verity said that she had not known that Peter had not told Bella and neither had I.

By this time tears were doing their usual track down my cheeks. I had got so used to crying I hardly even noticed it any more. But to my surprise, Verity, too, was visibly upset. At that moment I felt a womanly love for this pretty, neat little woman, this second wife. And for the first time I realised that sharing love for the same man gave us a bond. It gave us an opening to get on with each other.

'I'm so sorry, Verity. I'm so sorry.'

Verity said she was sorry too. She was sorry she hadn't come to see me earlier. But that it was only the other day that she wondered if there just might be some connection with this and Bella's disappearance. She said that whatever we had told Bella or not told her was our business, mine and Peter's, but she wished that she had known so that she could have been more careful.

Yes, I nodded. Yes, we, meaning Peter, should have told Bella that we, meaning Peter, was so ashamed of his own infertility that he did not want even Bella to know.

And, Yes, I agreed, it was not fair on Verity and it certainly was not fair on Bella.

I thanked her for coming over and telling me this. I even managed to ask her how she was feeling and how Sam was taking the news of having a new baby brother or sister. I got to tell her that well I for one was so happy for her and for Peter that they were going to have a child of their own. I got through another round of coffee with Verity, wishing her out the door, out of my house so that I could be alone with the huge mixture of feelings that were overwhelming me.

I wanted to be alone with my anger towards Peter. Bloody hell, why did we have to keep it such a secret? Just to protect his precious male pride! And why did I collude? Why did I feel so guilty about being normal that I would lie to my own child to protect his ego? And why hadn't he at least told Verity that Bella had never been told the truth?

As Verity was taking her neat little pregnant body out the door, I suddenly realised how horrible this must have been for my poor baby. My poor darling Bella. What have we stupid screwed up adults done to you?

I finished off the rest of the Tim-Tams for dinner and went out into the garden for a joint.

8. PETER

I have an urgency to see Peter.

I have an urgency to let him know how furious I am about what Verity has told me. But I also have an urgency for no more lies. I want to let him know as much as I do about Bella's safety. I can feel the war going on in my body. I know this war and I want instant resolution. But, I don't want to phone him the minute Verity gets out of my front door. She at least should be able to get home and then talk to Peter about it or not talk to Peter about it. That's her stuff.

'Breathe Gina, breathe', I tell myself.

I grab the opera disc that is on top of the pile. I put in on. Loud. I lie down on the floor and feel myself merge with the music swirling on the walls and the ceiling and I enter the tragic machinations of the singers, in wonderment, as I always am, at the sweetest of all instruments, the human voice, as it tells of human stories with emotions larger than life. And I focus on the blend of harmonies that are so exquisitely balanced that my head empties, and my heart fills, and the music pumps around my veins with the rhythm of my own heart.

The finale. I get up and phone Peter. The line is busy.

Since that first week, when Peter was around every night, we have been keeping a distance from each other. Only brief phone calls from him, asking if I had heard anything. I keep them brief. He makes me feel so guilty. He asks all these questions. What do the police say? What are they doing to find her? What am I doing to find her? What should he be doing? Why hasn't anyone responded to the posters? Should we put some more up? In different places? Should we be walking around with her photo, asking if anyone has seen this teenager? Offering rewards? I keep my cool with him. Of course he asks these questions. They are perfectly reasonable. It's just that I can't cope with them. OK Alma, it's crunch time. Look, I'm doing it.

I dial his number again and he answers. He sounds surprised to hear my voice. Have I heard? No, not yet. I tell him I want to see him. I can hear him scanning his busy schedule. Yes. Tomorrow. In the afternoon. Yes. Let's go for a walk. Yes. Let's meet at Bondi Beach. Yes. Outside the dressing sheds. Yes, four o'clock will be fine. I feel as though I have just done Bondi, with Teff. But OK. So what.

Bondi. It was, after all, our old playground, Peter's and mine. That is where we got to know each other. Did we really fall in love? Yes, I suppose so. It is so hard to imagine that, now. But Bondi is where we walked the beach, walked the promenade, ate fish and chips on the grass. Bondi is where we shared our dreams, made our plans, had our first fight, and our second, and our third. Hey, now that's not fair, I tell myself. We did have fights because we were feisty then. We had spirit. We had drive. We were going to make the whole world a better place, for our children, we said. We wanted to clean up the planet. We wanted to prevent any further wars. We wanted to bring back truth and the common good.

Stop it. I try to focus on what I want to say to Peter and how I can do it without frightening him off with what he calls hocus pocus. Do I tell him I know she is alive? Do I tell him I know that because she visits the house on Tuesdays, and I can smell her perfume in her room and we exchange gifts under her pillow? Great. Peter will really go for that one. But he's her father. He has the right to know she's alive. No, he's not her father. Yes he is.

Stop it. I try to picture myself as Peter and try to figure out what he could possibly hear from me that would reassure him.

Look, Peter, I'm sure in myself. Come over next Tuesday. What if she doesn't come? No. Perhaps I can just let him talk first.

I'm the first to arrive and I wait, outside the dressing sheds. It is a windy, cloudy afternoon. The southerly has kicked in and is whipping up white caps on the waves. I'm always on time. I can't help it. Actually, I'm always a bit early. Just in case, so I won't be late. If I think I'm going to be late I go into a panic. I hate being late. So I wait there, enjoying the scene. The joggers. The bladers. The power walkers plugged into their iPods swinging their weights, up down, up down. The gays, hand in hand. The anorexic girls in their skin tight black bike pants and tiny little midriff tops. The boys, swaggering. The old couples, walking, talking. What have they got left to talk about? And the sea. Breakers rolling in and crashing on the sand. How I love that sound.

He catches me by surprise.

'Gina!'

He gives me a hug. Do I look so in need of a hug? It feels good. He was always good at hugging. Although where he learnt if from I couldn't possibly guess, with his stiff uptight Christian family of his.

'Hi, Peter. My you're looking good.'

And he is. Time has been kind to Peter. His body has hardly aged, still tall and slim. He looks so clean. As clean and neat as Verity. But as I take a closer look I notice age lines around his eyes and his mouth. His forehead, always with a tendency to wrinkling has more permanent folds. I wonder if he will look like a Bassett hound when he gets older. I am reminded how hard this past month must have been for Peter, since Bella disappeared. I am reminded how hard it is for him right now. And

I remind myself that I have asked to meet him to talk about that. So I take first bite.

'I was wondering how you were coping Peter, since Bella left. I thought perhaps it would be a good idea for us to talk about things.'

He sighs. He's always been a great sigher, Peter. He sighs when he finishes a task, even sex. He sighs when he sits down and unfolds his newspaper. He sighs when he hangs up the phone. He sighs when he is under the shower. He sighs when he doesn't know what to say next. I know this man, his sigh reminds me.

I wait. This is very unusual for me. I hate silences. I rush in to squash them. I work on the principle that if you are not going to talk then I am. But tonight, I wait. And we fall into step. My God, I think, just like me and Teff. Me and Terry. Me and Peter. What is this walking with men? This is beginning to be a habit.

He sighs again, but this time it is a small one and I know it is the signal that the words will start coming soon. Peter has always found it hard to start, but once he's going he goes full on.

'Sometimes I think I will go mad. It is beyond me. Here we are two intelligent people and our teenage daughter has gone missing for nearly a month now and what have we heard? Nothing. Hardly a day goes by when I don't ring the police to ask if they have heard anything and if not, exactly what they are doing to find her. They say they are doing the usual things and they do take it seriously, but they also say the overwhelming stats are that kids just go missing for a while and then come home and that they have absolutely no reason to believe that she has been ….'

He cannot say that word. Neither can I.

'They say they have made all their enquiries at the school, with all her friends, traced her pathways to and from school, checked the hospitals, the rape centres, King's Cross and other places where street kids are known to hang out. Nothing. They say that thousands of kids run away each year, and they can't spend all their time trying to find them. They say that after all, she is sixteen.'

I wait for him to go on.

'She must be somewhere. Our little girl is somewhere. Why don't we know?'

This is so hard for me. I feel Peter's pain, like I used to feel his pain over so many other things. His pain about me not falling pregnant. His pain that it was him when he was so sure it must have been me. His pain at being passed over for promotions. His pain that I was such a wimp. And finally his pain that we fell out of love and our dream of happy families dissolved before our very eyes, and that I was the one who said I wanted more out of life than just existing together, like this.

And I feel his presence next to me and even though I know I made the right decision at the time, to get out before it went really bad, his presence feels familiar and reliable and predictable and I think he is a good man, Peter. He cannot help it that he got so boring and picky and depressed.

His questions still hang in the air, between us. Unanswered. A silence. Here I go.

'Peter, I know how you are feeling. It is terrible for you and it's terrible for me.'

I don't add that Bella is all I have. I don't say that at least you have Verity, and are starting another family. I don't add, at your age. And I don't, and I give myself credit for this, say anything about Verity's visit and Bella finding out so bluntly that you are not her biological father and let's look if that little shocker could have had anything to do with all this.

I decide to level with him. Despite it all, I owe him that much. He thinks I'm a nutter anyway so what do I have to lose?

'I want to tell you something. I want to tell you about something odd that has been happening and I think it has to do with Bella and it's her way of telling us that she is all right.'

He stops. He turns to look at me. He is pale. We silently walk off the promenade and head up the grassy slope. We sit down on the grass. It is getting colder as the sun starts its long exit by hiding behind the tall buildings facing the beach. We sit side by side, slightly huddled together and I try to explain.

'... so for the last two Tuesdays, when I get home from work, I go up to her room, and there is the fresh smell of her lavender oil, it's her Tasmanian lavender oil, I know, and then last Tuesday the money and the note I left under the pillow were gone and there was a little flower in its place. Peter. I know she has been. I know she is alive.'

It's a long time and many sighs before he manages, almost in a whisper,

'Well I don't.'

'Peter, do you remember about the little flowers? How every time you took her for a walk, even just to the shops, when she was little, how she always picked the tiniest flower she could find to bring home for me, and I had to float it in the lid of a medicine bottle to make her happy. It was a ritual. She even used to throw away the one she picked if she found a smaller one. Don't you remember? Who else knows about that? Who else other than you and me and Bella?'

More silence.

'Peter, do you remember when we left her for the first time, and took her over to Teff's and Mirium's for a week and had our first holiday on our own when she was three and we went to Tasmania and did that big Cradle Mountain walk and for some strange reason you decided to bring her back that little bottle of pinky – mauve coloured lavender oil because it was just the colour that she said was her favourite. Well she never lets herself run out of that oil. It's like her reminder that her Daddy brought her a special gift. She keeps it going. It smells different Peter. And I can smell it. On Tuesdays I can smell it.'

More silence.

Three sighs.

Then, 'So what do you reckon. She's run away from home for some unknown reason but she comes home once a week.'

'Yes.'

'Have you told the police this?'

'Hardly.

'Have you told anyone? Teff? Alma?'

'No'. I lie. He doesn't approve of all the money I spend on Alma.

'What would you say if I talked it over with Verity?'

'Peter, I think that would be a great idea.'

This reminds me of the other stuff I needed to talk to him about and I can feel the anger beginning to rise. I put it down with the promise it will get its turn. Later. I stick to the present.

I want to tell him that on a good day I am confident that Bella will come home soon. I want to tell him that Teff, too, said that he feels that she will. I want to share with Peter some of the hope I feel. I don't want to share with him my despair on my bad days, my incredible feeling of failure.

I hear him say, 'Will you phone me next Tuesday night? Will you phone me every Tuesday night? Will you phone me if you hear anything? Anything at all? Will you tell me everything about anything, even if you think I won't believe you? Will you Gina, will you, will you?'

I cannot answer. I am too choked up with tears. So I nod.

I am such a coward. I cannot bear to broach that other matter. I cannot scream at him, just what the fuck do you think you were doing having a conversation she could hear about you fathering a baby when you didn't father her.

Because while it was welling up to the surface demanding to be heard, I heard the other little voice of reason. He didn't exactly plan it that way, Gina. He's just been telling you what a rough time he's been having Gina. Will you just let it go, Gina.

I drive home still with tears welling up. A really stupid thing to do. I have made many promises to myself about not driving and crying at the same time. So I pull over and have a good mop up. Blow nose. Wipe eyes. Unwanted numbers come into my head but today they are strangely comforting. Bella is only three years younger than my mother when she ran away. It is as if I am understanding for the first time the hugeness of what my mother did when she ran away from her family. She ran half way across the globe. What is this telling me? No. I do not believe my Bella is pregnant. But is it something she believes in so strongly like my mother believed she had to leave Germany? Two strong Bella's. Both driven by their strong beliefs. Two survivors. Yes. I will hang onto to that one. My Bella is also a survivor. But I do not have a clue about what she is surviving.

I open the front door to the sound of the phone ringing. Instead of my usual habit of letting it ring out, I grab the receiver.

'Hi. It's Geoff. Gina, what's going on? You don't return my calls. I haven't seen you for weeks. How are you making out? Can I come over and see you?'

'Oh Geoff, I am so sorry. Not now. No, now's not such a great time. Thanks heaps for phoning, but, honestly, Geoff, I think I just need the weekend to myself.'

'So she's not back yet.'

'No'

'She will, love. She'll be back soon. You've got to stay positive."

'Ta. Thanks Geoff. I'll talk to you soon. Bye'

He should talk about positive, I mutter.

I put the receiver back on its cradle. Cradle. What a comforting thought. I go upstairs and lie down on my bed. I stick my thumb in my mouth and rock. I cradle myself. I shut out Peter's pain, and my pain, and Geoff reaching out in his own way, and the incredible mess our lives have become. I shut out everything but my thumb. Nobody can take away my thumb. Nobody can stop my rocking. Mercifully the room darkens and I fall asleep.

9. GINA

I wake up to find it is almost morning. Yes, it is Tuesday and I have survived five weeks of this nightmare. I just want to go back to sleep again. I am so tired of everything.

Last night Terry and I must have walked miles. We certainly stayed out for hours. So far these Monday nights with Terry suit me fine. He has dinner. I have dinner. Then I walk over the road to his place just as he and Bounce are coming out the gate. We don't even talk about where we are going to walk. We just walk.

Terry is beginning to open up more. Last week he told me that he had been married until a few years ago. He married an Irish woman. He had fallen in love with her during one of his visits to Ireland. He had met her at Trinity University in Dublin. She was a mature age student, and they started going out. Terry told me how they got married, on an impulse so that they didn't have to invite any of her family or his. She thought it would be fun to come to Australia. He found her exotic. Different. Every time she opened her mouth, he was transported by her deep and melodious voice. He kept conversations going just to hear it.

She did come to Australia, and they had a son, and then she got depressed and lonely and missed her family and friends. Terry said he doubts if they were really in love in the first place. Real love. Love past first infatuation. Anyway, she left and took the little boy, Brendan. He's six now, and Terry misses seeing him although he tries to go over once a year, and hopes that when Brendan is older he will be able to visit him in Australia. He doesn't really miss her. In fact, he hates her, now, for taking his child away. But there wasn't anything he could do.

So, he said, that's why he came over when he heard Bella was missing. That's how he knew that it would be hard for me. He didn't really mean to tell me about Brendan. He was sorry.

Sorry. I told him I was sorry. I really was sorry about Brendan. I was really sorry that Terry had lost so many precious times of his son's growing up. So now, in this pink dawn, I look across and can see that the light is still on in Terry's room I feel so sorry all over again. I have a whole new thing to feel sorry about. I feel so sorry for all the stuffed up kids and mums and dads and wonder what on earth is happening to our species. What on earth are we all doing to each other, inflicting pain, causing separation, causing loss? Separation is bad enough when it is a few suburbs away, but how would you cope with having your kid half the globe away? Where have we gone so wrong? And I drift back to sleep wondering if there are any normal people out there any more? Could I please start attracting into my life people who are happy? And the other voice, says, well Gina, just look at yourself. You can't stand people who are happy, just now. Drifting off back to sleep looks like a good option.

But I have one more thing to think of before I do that. I want to give myself some time to think about a part of my work I haven't shared with Terry yet. I don't tell too many people about this part. But it is beginning to worry me because it is beginning to get out of hand. And while I am reminded of "half mad with worry", I know that sometimes I am more than half mad, especially now with worry about Bella, and this is one mad that I am aware of. Sometimes I worry about the mad that I am not aware of, but I decide I can't worry about that at the moment. Besides. It's too hard. So it's back to worrying about what I really want to worry about now.

Most Fridays I get time out from the office to represent the department at a script conference for a soapie of all things. This soapie has been running for a few years now, on one of the commercial television stations. It is set in a country town in NSW called Wattle Bridge. It runs at prime viewing time from Monday to Thursday with a complete story for each week. Some of the characters are regulars and some are brought in just for one story.

One of the core families is a couple with grown up children who have been doing short term foster care ever since their own children were small. They are the main reason that I started to attend the script conferences. The script writers wanted to know how fostering worked, and how children became fostered and if they got to see their parents and how their parents ever got them back into their own care. Then they wanted to know what happened in other situations, like when the school teacher was found fondling teenagers, when the teenage girl got too pregnant for an abortion, when the couple who failed IVF wanted to adopt an overseas baby, and a host of other whens, and ifs, and buts. I was supposed to know all about these situations and more, but at least I know who to ask and in that way I make sure that I am useful at the script conference. Otherwise, I just make it up.

There are other consultant experts, as they call us, at the script conferences, from time to time, and we have all got to know each other quite well – the lawyer, the teacher, the police, the doctor and the clergyman. We enjoy each others' company and some of us have lunch together on Fridays, after the script conference. They know about Bella and are very supportive of me.

Over the past five weeks, since Bella went missing, my time falls into two simple categories. There is "safe" time and "unsafe" time. Safe time can be with one other person, like Teff, or Alma, or even my ex Peter. Terry gives me safe time. Time by myself can be very unsafe especially when my mind digs up really horrible scenarios about Bella. Even knowing that Bella comes on Tuesdays doesn't always stop the horror movies in my head. So I go into fog. Fog can be very comforting. I can disappear into it.

I spend a lot of my time in fog. Sometimes I open the fog and creep out, relate to someone, and then pop back in, where it is safe.

Strangely, script conferences are safe. I can creep out of my fog and get involved in the messes of other people's lives. And this little rural community certainly has messes! Mess after mess after mess. And I know how to make it messier! But I don't really get the chance to do that. They aren't my stories.

But lately I am not safe in this soapie script conference, because I am getting out of control with my suggestions for the script. I must ask Alma if this means I am finally losing it.

Since Bella left, I find myself thinking a lot about Belinda and Tom Cameron, key characters in this soapie, who have fostered more children than they have kept count of. They fascinate me. Actually, I hate Belinda and Tom Cameron. I really want them to trip up. I really want to suggest that the script writers raise the standards they have to reach as foster parents and keep raising them so high so that they fail, really badly, just once, with one really challenging kid. I want them to fail just like the real parents fail. And just like, a very tiny voice inside whispers to me, just like you have failed. You have failed, Gina. You have the most precious child and you have failed.

Sometimes I hate all the parents whose children have not run away. Some of them are much worse than me.

Belinda is overweight, cheerie, wears pink tracksuits and has a blonde pony tail which she ties high up to the centre of her head. She's not perfect. She's fat.

Tom is very thin. He too has a pony tail, which is now greyish and long and wispy. He ties it at the nape of his neck. Tom smokes rollies. There was a lot of resistance to this, in the script conferences, but the doctor finally gave in and acknowledged that a smoker could reinforce some good lessons about not smoking. So Tom's not perfect either.

One of the foster children is Eli. I feel partly responsible for him and his problems in life as I played an important part of making him up in the first place. It happened when I was asked the sort of things that could go wrong in a family with an adopted child. Well, I started to explain that most adoptions these days are for children born overseas, in countries like Korea, India, Sri Lanka, Columbia or China. They liked that, at the script conference, and settled on an Indian child because casting had a very talented young Indian boy who they were keen to slot into a soapie. He is seven years old, but very small and fine boned and could pass for much younger.

Young Eli, the young soapie Eli, came into foster care almost a year ago. He had been removed from his very middleclass adoptive family. At first they absolutely adored him, but when he was four, his adoptive mother found to her shock and delight that she was pregnant. After Polly's birth, things changed radically for poor little Eli. His adoptive mother started neglecting him. Serious neglect. The adoptive father was too ashamed to do anything about it. Eventually, Eli was placed for a few months with the Camerons, while the adoptive parents received psychiatric therapy and now a whole year has gone by. My contacts at work, in the adoptions branch, assured me that this does happen. That the adopted child gets rejected when the family get a big surprise that their natural child is on the way. And it tends to happen in overseas adoptions, because there aren't many other sorts.

So far so good for the soapie. There is a good bit of tension here and potential for lots more. Cross cultural tension adds extra spice. We have a short term placement with the wonder foster parents, Belinda and Tom which is stretching out way over time.

But the real Eli is not thriving. Something worries me about this child, this little seven year old who looks five. He is way too small for his age and his little legs are like sticks. Is this cultural? Is this what little Indian kids look like? He seems to have no interest in food. But is this only when he is on the set? How do I know what the kid eats in his real life? And now Eli's eyes have lost their lustre and sparkle and his hair has lost its usual sheen and hangs down limp over his eyes. But then why wouldn't he look washed out? He goes to school and then goes to rehearsals and shooting afterwards most days of the week. Wouldn't that tire out any seven year old, especially one with skinny legs who looks only five?

I get confused. I do not know whether the real child, the child actor who comes with his real parents, is a worry or if I am just getting him mixed up with the soapie kid in foster care who should be a worry. Sometimes I can't get a handle on the difference.

I find this very disturbing and have even talked to Alma about it. I thought she would tell me that I had enough to concentrate on, in my real life, without getting emotionally involved with a pretend child in a soapie, or a real child who is trying to be a pretend child in a soapie. But she was quite prepared to talk me through my feelings about Eli, and what he represented to me. She also led me through my confusion about my own role. OK. So I'll just advise them about what happens in real life cases and butt out of Eli's real life. Or, if I am really worried that the real Eli is in any way maltreated, then I should do what I keep telling people to do in the pamphlets I write, have a chat to the Mum, offer support, or, if I am really concerned, notify him to the department. But I know I am not going to do any of the above.

Well I have given Eli an hour or so of my precious early morning brain, I am not closer to solving any real or pretend problems and it is time to come out of my fog, comforting as it is.

Lately, when I come out of my fog I feel that I am tip-toe-ing along a cliff top. I have to be so careful not to fall off the edge hundreds of metres into the rough seas below. Just like, when we were kids, when we used to climb along the big cliffs between the beaches. Then we didn't give a care. But now I am super vigilant. I know I can slip without any warning.

And now I know that I am not alone on the cliff top. My brother Teff keeps sentry duty on top at the steepest part. He, too, is ever mindful of the danger. I see him flirting with the possibility of going down. I imagine him in free fall and the thud on the wet rocks below. But Teff doesn't let himself fall. He is supervigilant. For both of us.

Part of me knows that neither of us will really slip and fall. But both of us live out our lives with unnatural caution. Some inheritance, eh? How many generations will it take, Mama?

And where are you my precious baby? Are you tiptoeing along your own cliff face? Or are you running along the edge with the wind in your hair? Are you carefree and brave or are you afraid, like us, in case you fall into the turbulent waters of the irrational mind?

Don't stay there, my baby, testing yourself out. Please come back before it gets too hard.

I get up, shower and get dressed for work. I get through the day. Blessed fog.

I race home. A tiny red berry on a stalk. 'Try not to worry Mama. I love you so much. I will come home. But just not yet. Love you heaps, Bella.'

I do the right thing and leave Peter a message on his answering machine. I am so relieved I do not have to talk to him.

10. BELLA AND NICK

Bella keeps going, stoked by her thoughts for next Tuesday. She guards her Tuesday secrets. She thinks about them for hours before she goes to sleep at night. She fantasises letting herself into the house one day and finding her mother at home, in bed because she is sick, or because she has a lover, or because she needs to take a day off and wants to finish a novel. She sees herself, creeping up the stairs and then a "Hullo. Who is that?" coming from her mother's room and she sees herself leaping up the stairs two at a time and diving into bed with Gina and them smothering each other with kisses and hanging on tight to each other until they fall asleep. Entwined.

Bella has been working on her Tuesdays, making them as special as she can. She walks the two miles to the station, slowly. She has plenty of time. She waits for a train that stops at every station. It takes longer that way. Once she's in the city she goes to a café where the waitresses don't seem to notice she takes an hour to have a cup of coffee and a muffin and intensely reads the whole of the morning paper. Especially the jobs section. She's seen other people taking a long time over that. Sometimes she puts red circles around jobs that take her fancy.

As she walks around the Botanical Gardens, she plans that if it were raining she could go to the public library. She's never been. But she loves the look of the big stone steps and gothic columns. It looks important. It looks like it has every book in the world. She could take notes and look like a real student. But the most exciting time of the day, on Tuesdays, is when she gets off a train at Kings Cross station.

As she walks past the little front gardens in her street she keeps a lookout for a small flower to pick. She sees it. A tiny head of purple lantana flowers. She nips it off the bush with a deft movement, hardly stopping as she does it. She pulls off the minute florets from the flower head, until only one remains. She carefully lays it in the palm of her hand. She remembers the white clover flower, and then the red cotoneaster berry from last week. The remaining lantana trumpet is even tinier. She smiles, remembering the game she used to play with her dad. So far she is winning.

She puts a circle of light around herself. This protects her from being recognised by neighbours, local shop keepers, kids. But then, she is sure that most of the neighbours would not be home at this time of day. Hardly any of them have children. She often wonders why her parents chose to buy a terrace house in this neighbourhood. There are no children. It is hardly a neighbourhood at all.

She walks in her circle of white light right up to her house, with one hand holding the key tight and the other curled around the lantana flower. She lets herself in the front door and closes it carefully. And then she crumples, inside and out. Just falls apart, there in the lounge room of the little terrace house. Her eyes slowly pan the familiar room. The piano which fits under the stairs. The big wooden ball on top of the first post of the stair railing. She always rubs it for luck as she goes up the stairs. The wispy white curtains with rust marks on the bottom. The fluffy blue lounge where she has watched her favourite soapies. She walks into the kitchen, and even at this time of day, surprises the cockroaches playing in the sink. She starts to climb the stairs and goes up to the landing where she turns left into the spare room. She checks the ladder before she starts climbing the wooden rungs up and onto the floor of her bedroom in the roof space. She looks at her clothes, her ornaments, her photos on the wall, and flops down on the bed with a sigh. She closes her eyes and the red light in front of her shut eyes slowly clears to reveal her mother's face and the tears start streaming down her face, as she rolls over to muffle her sobs in her pillow. She reaches under the pillow and finds the envelope with two crisp $50 notes and the message that she is loved. She scribbles a brief hello to her mum, and puts her note and the little flower in the envelope under the pillow, puts the $100 in her pocket, and climbs down from her room, down the stairs, out of the house and into the bright sunlight. Whew.

On the train ride back to the city, she takes stock. Five weeks down and three to go until the day that they blow up the sperm bank at the hospital. They are now up to researching the hardest part. Explosives. She lets Nick's questions run through her head. What do you need to blow up a stainless steel freezer? Where is the best place to put the explosive? How long does the fuse have to be? How far away do you have to be so that you don't get hurt? It's so hard. How can she be sure she has all the right answers?

Then she starts her own questions. The ones she never has time for. The ones Nick doesn't think of because he doesn't care about these things. How do you make sure other people are that far away? What else will get damaged? The floor? What are the stress levels of the concrete floor the freezers sit on? What is on the floor underneath? She knows full well what is on the floor below. Premature babies. A whole ward of tiny little pre-term babies. She has seen them. They look hardly human with woolly hats covering their tiny heads, and tubes running in and out of every hole as well as doll sized arms and legs, and monitors wired from their bodies to machines which blip and draw graphs. But most of all she remembers their little chests going up and down, up and down, like there was an engine inside their little rib cages pumping the air in and out, in and out, and they kept doing that, all day and all night. Do they hurt, she wondered when she saw them. Do they feel pain, like we do? She remembers that there was something about them that revolted her, but she also remembers being aware of their immense will to live.

Bella feels sick. What if? What if they can't work it out properly? What if they do too much explosive? What if the floors are thinner than they think? What if the builders cheated and didn't put in as much re-inforcing as they should have? What if all those little bodies with their little chests pumping up and down suddenly got blown apart? Why hasn't she thought of this before? Is this what she sometimes wakes up screaming about in the night? Is she having dreams about the premmie babies on the floor below and it is too horrible to remember them? Why hasn't she thought about this before? Why hasn't Nick? He is the one who is supposed to keep the whole picture together. Nick, she recalls, is not travelling all that well himself anymore. Nick is popping more and more amphetamines and probably others things she doesn't even know about. Nick, Bella realises with a start, is not on top of things at all.

Bella could go back to Nick's right now. The cleaner is gone by lunch time. But Bella doesn't want to go back yet. She needs some time to think. She takes the train to Circular Quay and finds the Manly ferry wharf. It's the longest ride. She waits the half hour for the ferry and then gets swept into the ferry along with the river of other passengers. She sits down next to a window. She turns her body so that she doesn't have to see anyone and gets out a book and pretends to read. But there are people. There is a toddler in a pram, fretting and whinging.

There are kids eating from packets of chips, drinking from plastic bottles of water. There is a man sitting right next to her, opening his paper out wide so that his arm swings almost in front of her face. She cannot think.

She craves to be by herself. She gets to Manly and starts to walk along the beach. It starts to rain. OK, she thinks to herself. I'll go back to Nick's. She gets the ferry back into town, and another train, and by the time she gets there, it is time for Nick to be back from school. She lets herself into the big house and trips over the dog who has taken to lying across the hall at the front door, and goes straight upstairs to her room and locks the door.

Nick doesn't call out. She mumbles to herself 'Come to think of it his school bag wasn't in the hall. Perhaps he hasn't come straight home from school.'

'Bloody Hell,' she swears out loud. 'I don't care.' She wants to think, but she doesn't want to think about the premmie babies. Not yet.

Bella remembers that night when she overheard Verity and Peter talking and her first hints that Peter was not her biological father. She worked out for herself that she must have been a sperm donor baby. But perhaps she was wrong. Perhaps she doesn't belong here after all, with Nick, working out the plan for all the sperm donor kids. Perhaps her mum had an affair. Perhaps they had planned that she should have an affair so that they could have a child they could pretend was theirs. Perhaps her mum had an affair and then told Peter that they must have made a mistake, he could have kids after all.

Whatever it was, it must be really bad that no-one has told her. Because they're not like that. She can't remember ever finding out that her parents had lied to her. And she can remember the few times she got into really bad trouble was for lying.

No, there is something they are very ashamed about. Mum. Dad. Verity. Teff. All of them.

So if Verity and dad were telling the truth that night then one thing was true for sure, and that was that Peter wasn't really her father. So who is?

What a crazy family. Bella gets out a clean sheet of paper and her packet of felt pens. She props herself up on the bed and begins to draw, not a family tree, but a family tangle with names and connecting lines, some thick, some thin, some dotted. There is her and Gina with a fat red blood line. She adds Verity and Sam. Then she adds Peter with dotted blue lines to her and Sam. She puts in Teff, with a thin red line to Gina and a thin dotted line to herself. Then she adds her grandmother Bella with her lines to Teff and Gina, and to Teff's children and to her. But then she remembers that she should show that Gina and Teff had different fathers – and she puts more lines out to dead strangers to show that Teff never knew his real father and that Gina's real father never wanted to know her? What kind of a line is that? Perhaps, Bella thinks, the kind of line that her own donor father has to her. A not knowing line. Bella puts in a dot for Verity's new baby and grudgingly gives it a fat red blood line to Peter. And she wonders about having this new half-brother or half-sister and thinks it won't really be like having a real sibling. Bella reminds herself that she is almost old enough to be the baby's mother, and that there is no real line that she can draw between them. No blood lines. No step-siblings. No half siblings.

Bella feels the anger slip away and she is left with the tangled mess of threads which hold her family together and which also hold her family apart.

Most of all, she wants to know about the other half of herself. She knows about the Jewish part. She has heard stories of her namesake grandmother. And she knows her mother is Jewish, although Gina never did anything Jewish, and she knows she is Italian from Gina's father. She looks a bit Jewish. She looks a bit Italian. But what about the missing half? What about the part that she always thought was from Peter?

And if it was a sperm donor, who was that man, that medical student, that person who thought it was a good idea to donate his sperm? Was he that short of money? Or did he think he was so great that the world would be a better place with lots of his little offspring populating the globe?

She remembered her first suspicions that Peter wasn't her real father and that there was no-one she could talk to about this. She wanted so badly to talk to her mum and dad. But then, she realised, if her mum and dad wanted to talk about it, then they had plenty of time, like sixteen years.

It seemed so soppy to talk about it with her friends. Everyone has fantasies they got the wrong parents, but that usually happened somewhere in primary school, not when you were almost grown up. But then, at school, they started studying human reproduction, and fertility and sterility and how medical science had given people all sorts of programs, in vitro and ex vitro. They talked about all the different ways that sterile couples could be helped to have babies. They talked about the ethics. Was it OK to keep frozen embryos? Was it alright to harvest stem cells from embryos? Was it alright to be a surrogate mum? How about for your sister? How about with her partner's sperm? Who made up the rules like how many times you could donate sperm? And did they have to be tagged so that somewhere there was a list of where they went? And who decided to tell the kids or not to tell the kids and to set it up so that they could find their sperm source or their egg source if they ever wanted to know? They had a big discussion about it, at school. It got very heated. And then, all of a sudden, Nick got up and said that if there wasn't that sort of help, then he wouldn't be here at all, because his mother was fertilised by sperm donated to a sperm bank.

That caused a big silence and then a big stir. Kids asked him how he knew, and how was that for him, and if his dad who wasn't his dad acted differently from other dads. And some kids still kept on saying how it was immoral to muck about with nature and that if you couldn't have children then that was alright as there were too many people on the planet anyway. And then suddenly Nick got really angry and asked if they preferred he wasn't born. Well, he kept saying, he was born and he is here and what are they going to do about it now?

And then Mr Nichols stopped the discussion and said that it was good when there were different views and perhaps there was no right and wrong and that the main thing was that we had to learn to respect each other's views. But then, he always said that. Every time they got into a good discussion, he said that.

Bella remembers how she went up to Nick after school and told him that she thought he had been really brave. And then she told him that she had just found out about her own father. And that was how it started.

Bella could tell that Nick was still really angry although she could not quite get a handle on what exactly he was angry about. So the two of them walked off together towards the shopping mall and it was when they stood outside the video shop and saw a big poster of a new terrorist movie with figures running away from a giant explosion, and Nick stood still, staring at the poster and said,

'We are going to blow up the sperm bank.' And Bella did not know what to say, so she said nothing, and Nick thought, right, she's in.

Over the next few weeks Nick sought Bella out. Sometimes he walked to the railway station with her after school. He would ask her all sorts of questions about herself. Who she lived with. Where she lived. If her mum went out to work. What sort of work. Where her Dad lived. When she went to stay with him. He asked her why she travelled so far to go to this school. He told her that his parents, too, had picked it out as being special. He asked her about her favourite subjects. What she liked doing. At first Bella thought that he must like her, in a special sort of way, and was working up to asking her to go out with him. In a way, Bella was relieved when that didn't happen. She was curious about Nick, but had never fantasised about being with him.

Bella had never taken much notice of Nick up till now. He was a quiet one. One of the loners. Not exactly a nerd. He was too funny to be a nerd. Sometimes he would mutter very funny comments about what the teacher had just said, under his breath, so that only those who sat near him could hear him. Nick didn't seem to have close friends. He wasn't on any sporting teams, although he was the last speaker in the debating, and was really clever with what he could think up, all at the last minute. Bella often saw him walking between school and the railway station, but he caught the train home going north, while she always got the one going south.

Bella was curious about Nick. She wondered if she had heard him right when he said they would blow up the sperm bank. She didn't dare ask him in case it were true. But then it became ridiculously obvious it was true. He started to talk to her about her moving in when his parent left for overseas in a matter of a few days time. He said they would have to be very careful not to be seen too much together because people would remember when she went missing, and the police would want to speak with him. So he stopped being near her at school, and phoned every night from a public phone. Bella wasn't worried that her mother would notice, as Bella managed to keep the phone tied up most nights till her mother shouted for her to get off the phone and do her homework or go to bed. Nick sent her emails, which were in a sort of code, so that she thought she knew what he was talking about, but wished that she didn't. The longer this went on the more Bella got sucked in. Nick's energy and enthusiasm drew her in. Besides, she was a bit frightened of Nick. He took it for granted that she was as keen as he was. She didn't know how he would react if she pulled back now. She actually tried it once or twice, with a

'Well, I don't know Nick, if I can go along with all of this. Give me some time to think about it eh.'

And his reply

'We don't have time,' didn't leave her anywhere to go.

But there was something too, which resonated with Bella. Here she was, all on her own, thinking her family had played it straight with her all these years. Well they hadn't and she was angry about that. So why not do something absolutely outrageous? Why not go right over the top?

As it starts getting darker in her bedroom, Bella hears Nick come in through the front door, tripping over the dog, like her. She spares a moment's thought that even the dog is going mad. She calls out to him that she has a headache and is lying down. He calls back OK.

She closes her eyes and starts to picture that floor of the hospital at night with ts empty corridors, the sperm freezer room, the offices and the control room with its panels of blipping red lights. And then her mind drops down a floor she sees the rows of humidicribs, each with a tiny baby. And she sees the rush and movement of all the people, mothers, nurses, fathers, doctors, pathologists, X-ray technicians, hovering, doing, adjusting, patting, wiping, cooing, coaxing, breathing with, breathing for, willing for the feed to stay down, the chest to keep moving, for the baby to still be there tomorrow.

Bella sits bold upright. She leaps off the bed. She runs down the stairs, two at a time. She runs into the lounge room. She flicks off the TV. She screams

'Nick! We got to talk. Yeah, now.'

11. GINA

Week five is finally over. I am still here. Bella is still out there somewhere. Sometimes I am so angry at her for playing this game with me. Running away and not running away. Letting me know she is still here and not letting me know what she is doing or why. I still visit the police, but not quite so regularly now. Perhaps every second day, or sometimes two whole days go by and I haven't even been on the phone to them. I think they can tell there is a shift. Well, I have lost that sense of desperation. Perhaps they think I am getting used to the idea that my little girl has run off. They tell me that the case is still open. But then so are the few thousand other teenagers' files. They told me last time I was there that there must be an epidemic or something because so many more kids seem to be taking off.

Sometimes I spare a thought for the parents of these other few thousand teenagers whose kids don't wear distinctive perfume, come to the house once a week, deposit some tiny little flower and take off again with $100 to get them through the week. These other parents must be out of their brains with worry. But then, I wonder too, about all the situations some of these kids are running away from, the ongoing sexual abuse, the emotional neglect and all the other horrible things that adults do to kids.

But even knowing that she is all right, this is still wearing me down. Last night, I could hardly drag my feet to keep up with Terry and Bounce. Terry commented on how I'd changed pace from the week before, and was I giving Bounce's little legs a break. It didn't seem such a bad idea to agree that this was my main thought in life. Terry looked at my face and went quiet. My face shows. If I am happy it shows. If I am depressed it shows. I can never get away with pretending. It's not fair. I felt so grateful to Terry that I could just be me without any questions or probing or judgements and I guess Bounce was also grateful, not that she would let on about that.

To make up for the slow pace, we walked far that night. It was good for me, to tire myself out. He just started rambling on about his students at university and how so many of them arrive barely literate. And he pretended that I would be really interested in this. And of course I pretended I was, and even started asking questions, like, so what is different with kids leaving school now, compared to our lot, when we started uni. And I slipped into my old pattern of paying attention, and listening and talking with just a very small part of my brain, with the rest of my brain safely tucked away in the fog.

This morning I wake early. I jump up and clean the house before work. Mainly because I have not done much over the past few weeks and, as stupid as it sounds, I want it looking nice for Bella. For when Bella does come home. I pick a large vase of greenery with my one garden flower for the dining table. I take great care with the message in the envelope. I change pillow slip before putting the last touches to her room. I smooth the bedcover, plump up the pillow. Straighten the mirror.

And Yes. Bingo! After work. A tiny single flower from a ground cover daisy. And a message on the envelope in Bella's writing.

"Hi Mum, I hope you and Peter are OK. I'm heaps sorry if I have been giving you a bad time. I'm OK. It won't be long now."

I raced downstairs and phoned Peter. He said that he thought we should take the note to the police.

"No way!" I screamed down the phone. "No way." I could not for the life of me understand why Peter wanted to take it to the police and I equally couldn't understand why I was so against it. I guess I we both understood at some level that we were somewhat unhinged. He actually said, "Gina, I think we should but I can see that this would be too hard for you, right now." I silently thanked Peter, or Verity, or just time, for the changes in Peter.

This week is really dragging. My session with Alma helped. She believes me that Bella is alive and present, and that she comes to the house. The fourth week in a row seemed to clinch it with her. Alma had me imagine Bella coming home. I had to set the scene, like me coming home from work and finding her. And then what would I do? Alma offered to play Bella. This was good. It made me realise that I had to be careful of where Bella was at, and since I had no idea, I had to look for some clues. How did she look? How did she sound? Was she defiant, apologetic, contrite? I had to be the grown up and step outside my need to know everything at once.

I did a lot of thinking on Thursday night and was beginning to feel strong. Until Friday's script conference, which was a total disaster. Why couldn't they be doing episodes which didn't need my pretend expertise, like when the organic farm was contaminated and like when the local hero footballer came out gay.

But things are really hotting up at the Camerons. Strangely, Mary, the chief script writer, has turned on her precious Camerons. And it is all because of Eli. She wants to know if there are some children for whom all placements go wrong. Yes, I tell them. Yes, lots of kids have an average of one placement per year because each of them "go wrong". She wants to know if happens that a kid can get abused or neglected in foster care. And, yes, I tell them, that can happen. That does happen.

I definitely do not want to be there any more. Much as I had fantasised about things going wrong for the Camerons, I really do not want this reality played out in a few million living rooms.

'No'. I say. 'Not Eli'.

Mary coolly reminds me that I do not make up the scripts. Mary reminds me that I seem to forget that, a bit too often.

There is silence. All eyes around the table are going from my face to Mary's, back to my face, waiting for a reply.

And I do a really un-me thing. I stand up and say I am really sorry that this had to be last script conference and that I am sorry that it is at such short notice but my work load has gone way up and I can no longer afford this chunk of time nearly every week.

And I start to walk out, and everyone calls out goodbye and thanks and goodluck and I just go to my car feeling that a load has lifted. What load? I really don't want that little boy playing a role of being abused or neglected. I really don't want that little boy put under any strain at all. I really want Eli written out of that stupid soapie. And if he is there, then I want no part of it. They can pick someone else's brains.

★★★

That night I can't sleep. I lie awake listening to the sounds from the two small hotels which are close to my house. It is unseasonably warm for a winter night, and I have opened the double doors which lead out onto my tiny balcony. The light sea breeze comes in bringing with it the sounds of humans.

I feel comforted by Terry's light across the street. It's on. And his bedroom doors are open onto his balcony. He can hear the same sounds as I can.

Every now and again someone's voice rises above the collective buzz. A sharp laugh. A deep guffaw. A shriek of "O no!" Now the sounds are getting louder. It is closing time. There will soon be car doors slamming. Loud goodbyes. Motors revving. Sports cars. Yuppie cars. BMW cars. Urgently needing muffler repair cars. Horns that honk three notes. More shouts. Screams of tortured rubber tyres. Then, I say a silent thank you to the God of Closing Time. It's quiet again now, except for the usual hum of traffic and the odd truck.

It is midnight and I am still wide awake but dry eyed. It took a long time before I could lie in this bed and be dry eyed. I count this as one of my achieved goals. After Peter and I split up. I used to feel intense physical pain as I lay here on this bed. I used lie right here sobbing out my victim status. Poor me. Lucky them, whoever they were, making such a lot of noise in the pub. How pathetic.

It took me a long time to realise that, on the weekends Bella went to Peter's, I didn't have to go out at all. So I did the "Hey I can enjoy staying at home" phase. This was followed by an exhausting "Hey I can go to parties and pick up a one night stand" phase which was followed by the "I don't have to go to parties if I don't want to" phase. It took a couple of years for me to get to the phase where I could take on a lover for more than one night. I remind myself that I haven't seen my current married lover for quite some time now. Like my other friends whom I also haven't seen since Bella disappeared, he rings to see how I'm getting on and last time, he even suggested we spend a weekend on the boat.

I'm lying here regretting that I refused that offer. I could do with a weekend away from my life, and of course, some physical contact with Geoff.

I smile as I remember how I first met Geoff. It was through Ron. I remember the dying months of my relationship with Peter, and how we saw a lot of Lisa and Ron who were going through the same thing. The four of us had been hanging together quite a while, me and Lisa having long intense talks about our marriages falling apart, while our same aged children played innocently in our intensely emotional space. Ron and Peter sought comfort in each others' presence talking about everything except their marriages falling apart, except sometimes I would hear one say something like, "Women, I'll never understand them", and the other nodding with sympathy. One night when the four of us were playing scrabble, Ron stood up and paced the room, saying that he'd have to get some physical action going in his life, and suggested we all play squash or tennis once a week instead of bloody scrabble, and while Peter and Lisa pulled faces at the thought, I said, "why not?" And surprisingly Peter backed me up, telling Ron that I used to be the meanest thing on a squash court that he had ever come across.

And so it happened. One night a week at the Bronte squash courts. A full hour of wham, bam. At first it nearly killed me, but I as I got fitter and stronger, I got back to that wonderful feeling of power. Two people in a long narrow concrete pit, sending each other running and stretching for a speedy small black rubber ball, as it ricoched from racquet to wall to floor to racquet.

I can't remember when it started or who started it, but during one match I was playing with Ron, at some time I thought I heard Ron whisper a vicious 'Lisa' as he smashed into the ball, and I hit back with a tentative 'Peter', and he ran and reached out his racquet with a slightly louder 'Lisa' and I kept the ball going with a firmer 'Peter' and the rally got longer and longer and the Lisas and Peters got louder and louder as I struggled to get every ball, hoping against hope that Ron would miss his return, but he didn't and I had to keep going and going and going, until I was screaming Peter's name as I furiously lunged for the ball until finally crimson faced and breathless we fell in a huddle on the floor of the squash courts, lying on each other's gasping, heaving, sweaty bodies. We started to attract a crowd on Thursday nights at Bronte.

One evening, as we were slowly rehydrating with lemon squashes, Ron called over a friend he caught sight of.

'Geoff,' he said, 'I'd like you to meet Gina.'

'Hi Gina, I've seen you around here a few times,' he said, poker faced.

I blushed. As I looked up into his face I saw one of the most truly beautiful males I had ever set eyes on. I tried one of my most sincere smiles. His face crinkled into a grin, except for his eyes. I recognised him as one of us. One like me and Peter and Lisa and Ron. Another casualty of a failing marriage.

'Please join us.' And he did.

I didn't see him again until Peter and I had finally separated. He was still living with Anna. He is still living with Anna. This is still an ongoing problem for me. Geoff is my lover, but he is still Anna's husband. And his eyes have gone even sadder.

The phone rings. I jump out of my memories. I pick up before it can complete its first ring. 'Yes?'

'Hi Gina, it's Geoff.' OK it's not about Bella. It's Geoff.

'Gina.' He almost sighs my name.

'Yes?'

'Did I wake you?'

'No. It's OK.'

'Can I talk to you?' I hear the uncertainty in his voice.

'Sure, now? On the phone? Do you want to come over?'

'No, first I want to talk to you, right now, on the phone, and then I might come over, if it's alright.'

'Yes. What is it?'

'I've been doing a lot of thinking. When you said you wouldn't come away with me this weekend, I was so angry at you. I never really wanted to see you again. And I was feeling so sorry for myself. So I though I'd go on the boat anyway. And I did. But last night, there I was listening to the lapping of the water and feeling so horny and so rejected, and I began to really think for the first time that if my life was such a big mess and I tried to get a handle on what I was doing that was so wrong. So I started to put it down on paper and tried really honestly to look at the me and Anna thing. And the me and you thing. And the kids. And my job. And my unreasonable boss. And I tried to look at the ropes, you know, that keep me in spaces I don't want to be, and I started looking at what happens to me when I tug at the ropes and they just get tighter and tighter. Gina, is this making any sense?'

'Yes. Go on.'

I am wide awake and alert now.

"And for the first time, I tried to stay with that. I tried to stay with feeling of being all trussed up and why the fuck I stay there."

'And?' I ask.

'Gina, I feel terrible'

I try to focus on Geoff feeling terrible, and just manage a 'Go on.'

'Terrible because I feel so netted in. Like if I could create it then I should be able to uncreate it. But I don't know how to fix things up. All I seem to know is how to make more mess.'

'Where are you?'

'I'm walking along Oxford Street, using my mobile. I feel like I've been walking since last night. Perhaps I have. I don't think I've been home. I don't want to go home. I want to be with you.'

'So be with me. So come over.'

I put down the phone. I do not want to be a counsellor to Geoff. I want to hear him out, hear out how he is feeling and then leave it up to him to work out what to do about it. This mess that Geoff is in has not been without its advantages for Geoff. He has a family and a lover and so far he can have the lot. Lots of people don't even have one of those.

But I am glad that Geoff is finally getting some insight into how he is feeling about what he is doing. I think this is the first time I have ever heard Geoff talk about feeling anything at all. He usually talks about what he thinks.

I try to look at what I really want, with Geoff. It doesn't take long. I like the intimacy that comes with having a lover, even if I get the left over bits, after his wife and children. I love the sex with Geoff, the wonderfully long and exciting orgasms. I love sleeping with my tummy in the small of his back. I love waking up in the morning and finding that he is still there.

Right now, I love that tingling feeling in my body, that anticipation of his presence, that spark that we both feel when our bodies are close.

I pull out my only sexy nightie. I brush my hair. I clean my teeth. I light a candle. I find some massage oil and put it next to the bed. I run downstairs let the front door off the latch. I put two wine glasses and a corkscrew and a bottle of red on a tray, carry it upstairs and stow it under the bed. I fluff up the pillows and lie back with a smile on my face. I hope they hear me loud and clear, next door.

I feel complete for the first time in many months. I feel balanced on my five legged stool. I feel supported by Alma, by Teff, even by Peter, in his own way, by Terry and tonight, by Geoff. My big Bella wound is closing over. Sore, yes, but not gaping. Not tonight.

12. NICK AND BELLA

Nick is alarmed by the tone of Bella's voice as she runs down the stairs, demanding to have a meeting.

Nick is tired. It has been a big day at school. He was sent to the school counsellor because he kept falling asleep in class. He had to stay bright and alert and tell the councillor that, No, he was not having a hard time with his parents away, and Yes, his brother Chris was looking after him OK although he did throw in that they had been having a few fights lately, just to make it seem real. No, he was eating and sleeping OK, and No he wasn't worried about anything in particular, but he was finding his maths a bit difficult at the moment, and realised that he needed to keep up with his homework. Yes, he had been letting that slip a bit lately. Yes, he was getting on well with his friends at school, and No, he hadn't been out much lately, but he was used to having weeks like that, when he liked to be by himself more, but that he could feel it was already passing and he was making arrangements for next weekend.

And now he would have to deal with Bella. Boy, did she sound wound up about something.

They sit in the kitchen, at the table. Bella gets out the chocolate milk and two glasses and puts out a plate of biscuits. She waits for Nick to sit down, dreading what she is going to say, and not knowing how to say it.

'Nick. I want out.'

'You can't.'

'Yes, listen to me. I want out.'

Nick gets up and starts going out the kitchen door.

'You can't', he shouts back over his shoulder.

Bella screams at him to sit down and hear her out.

Reluctantly, he comes back to the table, but stands behind his chair, towering over her, his face deathly pale.

'Nick. It's the babies. We might kill the premmy babies.'

Bella notices that Nick has a very strange look on his face.

'We don't know enough', she goes on, 'and we won't ever know enough about all sorts of things so we can never be sure that we won't hurt them, or even kill them.'

'You don't know enough', he screams at her, 'because you haven't found out enough. You have to find out more and more and more till you have found out enough. That is your job. I do my job and it looks like you just can't do yours well enough.'

By now Bella is shouting too.

'Well, I can't. It doesn't matter how sure you are that we have the right amount of explosive, and how sure you are that the building is strong enough to keep the explosion to the sperm bank, I don't know that Nick, and I'm not going to do it.'

Nick stands there, pointing his finger at her, almost spitting at her in his rage. Nick is no longer real. In his anger his breathing is shallow and raspy. His face is red and the red is spreading down his neck where his veins are standing out in knots. He starts hyperventilating and with every huff and puff he looks more and more toadlike, his body getting redder and his veins getting knottier until they look like they will burst and splatter his blood all over the moulded ceiling of the stainless steel kitchen of his parents' house.

'But you said you would. You said you would do it. I could have got someone else. But it's too late now. You have to do it and that's all.'

Bella pushes past him. She races up to her room. She needs time to think. She needs to plan her exit. She does not want to leave Nick like this, angry and all alone. And she feels bad, because she did say she would do it. All along, she let Nick believe that they would plan this thing together, and they would do it together, no matter what.

And did she hear it right? Did she hear, as she raced past him and up the stairs, and into her room, did she hear him say,

'I'll kill you!'

It is then that she hears the click, closing the lock, on the outside of the door. She hasn't even noticed there was a lock. She is trapped.

Bella screams out at him.

'Open the door Nick.'

Nothing.

'Nick, let me out.'

Nothing.

'Nick, can you hear me?'

Nothing.

Bella lies down on the bed, her eyes fixed on the ceiling, and feels the fear creeping along her skin. She wraps her arms tightly around herself, and keeps her eyes on the ceiling, letting the sobs come out of her body in big gulping noises. For the first time in her life, Bella is very scarred.

She must have fallen asleep. She wakes, cold and hungry, in the dark. The house is deathly quiet. She puts aside her rising fears and concentrates on what she is going to do. She wants to talk to Nick about it some more, try to make him see that they have to stop the plan. Do it calmly and rationally, but she realises that there is no chance for that. Not now. She so hopes that he goes to school tomorrow. She desperately needs him to go to school tomorrow. She will need the time and space to work out how to get out of the bedroom. She does not dare to get started tonight. She won't even turn on the light and have a good look at the lock tonight. Even in her fear and panic she is curious about the bedroom doors locking from the outside. But then she remembered.

She remembered that when she first arrived at Nick's house, she used to ask Nick about his parents and what sort of things his family used to do when he was little, but Bella gave up asking as she never got any answers. But one night, when they had taken some time off and were watching some DVDs late into the night, they curled up together on the lounge, which was pretty unusual.

When Nick first asked Bella to come and stay at his house, she thought he would come on to her. She thought he must have found her attractive. But nothing did happen. While she didn't especially find Nick attractive either, she was quite disappointed that Nick didn't even seem to notice that she was a girl. Very soon it was clear. Bella was there for one purpose. Nick needed someone else to help him fulfil his plan.

So when they did get physically close, it was just like cuddling up to a friend.

That night, when they were watching videos, Nick started to talk about how he and Chris hated being locked in their rooms. Bella found this hard to imagine as she had never been locked in or out of anywhere. But, it seemed that when Nick was only a toddler his mother used to have long bouts of getting very drunk, and she would get violent, and so their father would to lock them in their rooms, he said, for their own safety. But Nick said he never felt safe locked away. He felt trapped. He said he would have much rather taken his chances with his mother's alcoholic rages and violence and anyway he wasn't all that sure that his Dad was right when he said she couldn't manage to flick open the locks when she was 'sick'.

Nick said that he and Chris stopped being locked in their rooms when their mother went away for what seemed like such a long time, and after that there was no more drinking, no more violence. Just quiet and sadness.

Now, Bella is feeling very trapped indeed. She knows how far it is down from the window. She has gazed out of that window so many times in the past month. She also looks at the possibility of sending an email or texting someone. Except she thinks her phone battery is flat and the charger is downstairs. Using her phone has been banned.

Somehow she goes back to sleep and wakes up to the sound of the front door shutting. She hopes Nick has gone to school after all. The time fits. The digital bedside clock says 8.10, the time he leaves every morning. She wonders what he thinks he is doing. Does he intend to keep her there all day, all night, for weeks?

Bella gets up, thankful for the many bathrooms in this house and that one of them is off the bedroom she is using. She examines the bedroom door lock. It looks pretty strong. She remembers the little trick she has read about in children's adventure stories, about sliding the piece of paper under the door and forcing the key out of the lock onto the paper with a bobby pin. But this door does not have a key, it just has a lever. And anyway, who has bobby pins? She checks the door itself, but it is solid. She checks the hinges, and thinks that this might be a possibility. If she could get the hinges off, then …

Bella throws open the window wide. It isn't that far to the garden below. And she works out that if she screws up the doona and the spare doona, she could drop them all out of the window onto the garden bed below, and throw down her pillow and the spare pillows as well. Yes, this looks like the best option.

Bella gets dressed. She puts her few spare clothes and her few other things into her bag and starts throwing all the bedclothes out the window. She throws her shoes down, and her bag. And then she climbs onto the window sill and looks down to the bedding below.

It looks a lot further down to the ground. She feels sick. But there is no choice now. Her bag and shoes are down there and she is up here. She knows Nick must still be out. She is quite sure she would have heard if he had sneaked back into the house. At least she hopes she is sure.

Bella pushes herself off the window sill, and let herself fall the four metres to the bedding below. She remembered to land on her shoulder and to immediately roll on impact. Her shoulder hurts but she wiggles it around and it works fine. She dusts the leaves and dirt off her clothes, puts her feet in her shoes, picks up her bag and walks, makes herself walk, not run, down the side garden, out into the front yard, down the pebble walkway to the front gate and out into the street

Bella sits in the train. This time she wants it to speed. She wants it rush through the northern suburbs, over the bridge and under the city, where she can change trains for home.

She clutches her bag tightly on her lap. She holds it like it is the only real thing in the world.

She hates Nick. She hates him for having that stupid idea. She hates herself for going along with it and then not being able to cope. She hates Peter for not having enough of the right stuff in the first place. She hates Gina for keeping the secret. She hates Verity for getting pregnant. How come there were enough sperm for her egg? She hates and hates and the more she hates the more she sees herself in the middle, caught in a web of all their treacheries against her.

But then the image of Nick coming home to the empty house fills her mind. She starts to feel genuine fear for Nick, and shame and blame for herself.

After all, she went along with the whole thing, didn't she? She acted like she was really going to last the distance, didn't she? She has failed Nick. She has failed everyone. Suddenly the whole thing looks like a really stupid thing to do. She has hurt so many people. And for what? Bella starts to feel bad about her mother, and her father, and Verity, and little Sam, and uncle Teff, and her friends who she has not seen for five weeks and who did not know that she was at Nick's all the time. Bella does not know how she can face any of them, any one of them.

Bella sits in the train, clutching her bag, and starts to cry. She is sucking in air, noisily. She is letting it out, noisily. She shuts her eyes so that she cannot see the people staring at her, or turning their backs on her. She just sits there and howls.

She opens her eyes to a slit when the train stops so that she can read the stations. She gets off at Town Hall, and still sobbing loudly, she makes her way up the escalators, crosses the station and then goes down, down to her platform. She no longer cares that people are staring. She can hardly see. She hears her train coming along side.

The image of Nick keeps appearing before her eyes. Bella knows that she should not have left Nick there, by himself, in the big house. But she also knows that she cannot go back. She turns her back on the train and finds the up escalator at the station her eyes scanning for a public phone. All she can see is people on their mobiles. She overhears some of the conversation. "Hi, I'm at Town Hall Station, so I will be a bit late." "What are you up to?" "Really! Noooo." She wants to rip a mobile out of someone's hand. Finally she finds the public phone. Digs her phone book out of her bag. Finds Nick brother Chris's phone number. Finds coins. Dials. It rings. She taps her foot. Answer. A message bank.

'Hi Chris. It's Nick's friend Bella here. How about going around and seeing if Nick is OK. I am a bit worried about him.' Feeling that was a really stupid message, Bella doesn't know what else to do. She races down the stairwell of the railway station. Back to her platform. This time she has to wait. It seems like forever before a train pulls in. The doors open with a big sigh and then shut again behind her. She stands this time, swaying with one hand curled around a stainless steel pole and the other still clutching her bag, and she leans her head against the cool metal, and listens as her gulping sobbing fades, and she silently counts the stations, one, two, until she knows she is almost home.

Bella lets herself into the house. Her mother is not home from work yet. Soon. Bella lies down on the blue velvet lounge. She uses one of the cushions as a pillow. She shuts her eyes and falls blissfully asleep.

★★★

It is late. I have been to see Alma after work.

We talked about how depressed I was getting about this Bella business. This knowing and not knowing. But most of all not having. I so desperately want her back. I want her in the house. I want to know she is safe because she is with me. I want to stop worrying. I want to sleep at night knowing she is here and I want to wake up in the morning knowing she is in her bed, upstairs, in the roof.

Alma listens, nods, passes the Kleenex box and lets me say it all.

Then, she starts probing. She gets out her longest and most penetrating probe and starts lifting the lid I have placed firmly shut on the supports I could be allowing in and am obviously choosing not to.

Where are my friends?

I want to shout – None of your bloody business.

I give myself a few minutes' stay of proceedings by wondering who in their right mind would pay money to someone to do this to you. Then I remind myself – no-one. That is no-one in their right mind. I am not in my right mind. My mind is a mess. My life is a mess. Which is why I am seeing Alma in the first place. And, I have to admit to my disturbingly questioning other self, this is why I am here. It is hard and it is expensive but it is making a difference.

I try to explain to Alma that my weekly sessions with her give me what I need in talking about Bella. She listens. She understands. She does not judge me as a terrible mother who has driven my daughter away. She accepts me with all my shortfalls, and she, more than anyone else knows about them. All of them. Well, almost all of them.

Tell me about what is happening with any of your friends, she says. Are you seeing any of them? Tell me about that.

I tell her that they leave messages on my answering machine. I tell her that at first I couldn't return them because ... well I can't remember exactly why, but it had to do with feeling so inadequate. Especially .. and.. whose kids were doing so well. And as the weeks went passed and I kept getting their messages, it got harder and harder to make contact. And they started leaving me "outs" ... said things like she understood if it was too hard to phone back but when I was ready she would love to see me, and .. stopped leaving messages at all … But I miss them I really do. I miss our weekly coffee sessions one morning before work. I miss going to the movies with ….

Alma lets me go on and on. As she listens I listen to myself and it all sounds so pathetic. So lame. For goodness sakes. They are my friends. My sisters.

It feels safer for me, at the moment, with men. Peter and I are able to give each other support at the moment, in a way we never could when we were together. We share this pain and we are kind to each other. Teff, of course, is always there for me. And Terry. So unenquiring. No probes. No need to ask questions. Just is. And I am not at all sure about Geoff, just as I never really have been.

And I come to realise that I keep my women friends at a distance because they do probe. They do ask questions. Really good questions. They do it out of kindness and concern, just like I do when one of them is having a rough time. And I realise and I say it out loud to Alma, that I want them back.

And she says that I can see them and I can tell them what I need and what I don't need, just like one of them could tell me.

OK. I have some homework from this session. I will start with … tonight. One phone call. That's all. Have a chat and make an arrangement. Not so hard? No, not so hard.

I am tired in my bones. I let myself into the house and I reach up to turn on the light. I stop, with my arm midway up, still clutching the keys. I can smell lavender oil. I leave the front door open so that some of the street light shines in the front door. There on the blue velvet lounge is a sleeping figure, curled up tight, embryonic. I slowly and carefully move closer and closer, trembling with excitement, doubting my own eyes.

It is Bella. Hey, It's Bella. I drop down on the floor beside her. I allow my hand to reach out and touch her beautiful hair, the side of her face, the curve of her neck. She is so warm. She is breathing deeply, fast asleep. I sit there, half kneeling on the floor, patting her hair, comforting us both with soothing noises which come from deep down in my throat. My mind goes into a glorious state of neutral. Empty. No thoughts. She is. I am.

She stirs and shivers slightly. I quietly get up and go upstairs for a blanket which I carefully place over her, shushing and hushing all the while. I shut the front door. I creep into the kitchen and put on some hot water for tea. I phone Peter. I phone Teff. I phone Alma, I phone Geoff. Last I phone the police. I make my tea and take it into the lounge room. I plonk myself down in the chair opposite the lounge. I am there for the long haul. She is not going out of my sight.

It is late at night and I am stiff, cold and hungry. I creep into the kitchen and put a mess of food into a saucepan. A tin of baked beans. Chilli sauce. Chopped up fetta cheese. Left over cooked broccoli. While it heats I creep up to the spare room and lug the mattress off the bed, and struggle with it as I try to push it down the curves of the stairs to the lounge-room. I check Bella. She is still there. Breathing. I race back up the stairs and grab some bedding and my book and dump them on the mattress. I check Bella. She is still there. I race back upstairs to the toilet. Hurry. Hurry. Back down the stairs. Grab the saucepan just before the whole mess starts catching on the bottom, grab a spoon, and I curl up on the mattress, eating greedily straight from the saucepan. Ahh. I risk turning on a small table light to read by. I take off most of my clothes, lie down on the mattress and try to read. I jump up and change the message on the answering machine.

'Hi this is Gina. Bella is home. We are both sleeping. Please leave a message.'

I turn the volume down as low as it will go. I lie back on the mattress.

Very soon, I too am fast asleep.

13. HOME

Over the next few days we slip into a very strange pattern of living. I take two weeks leave from work. I bless my boss for understanding and make meaningless promises that I will make it up, somehow, someday.

Bella slowly uncurls from her foetal position and leaves the blue velvet lounge for essential activities like going to the toilet. The rest of the time she and the lounge have merged into one. She lives on vegemite toast and cups of hot chocolate. This has pretty much become my staple diet too. It is not bad. It is very comforting. It does not take very much time to prepare, and I can slip up to the corner shop for bread and milk almost any time of the day or night. We watch a lot of soapies together on the TV and daytime quiz shows. We wake up in the middle of the night and watch very bad movies and have more vegemite toast and hot chocolate.

Our conversations are very short and few and far between.

Bella: I'm not going back to that school, Mum

Me: No. That's OK.

Me: Peter rang and wants to come over tonight after work, just for a few minutes.

Bella: Not yet Mum.

Bella: I want to tell you about it all, but not just yet Mum.

Me: No? That's OK.

Bella: I want you to take the mattress back upstairs. You can sleep in your own bed. I'm not leaving here.

Me: OK

Me: I thought I might make a soup tonight.

Bella: Whatever.

But it is not OK. The big questions are screaming silently inside my brain. Where have you been? Why? What have you been doing? Why? Why are you like this? Why? When are you going to get off that fucking lounge and start behaving like a normal person? How long can I keep it up? What about me?

So eventually I say,

'Bella. I would like you to get up now and have a shower. Get into some clean clothes, and we'll drive down to the beach for a walk. And we'll buy fish and chips and we'll sit on the grass and you will start telling me what has been happening with you.'

And she says 'OK'.

While she is showering, I leap up. I strip the lounge of its sheets and blankets. I throw the cushions off the lounge and pound them with my fists before throwing them back. I scoop up the bedding and dump it in the washing machine. I race upstairs and scoop up the heap of clothing she has walked out of and throw all of that in the washing machine too. I tear my own clothes off as well and dump them in the machine. I throw in laundry powder and flick the dial round to start. I race upstairs naked into my room and lay out clean jeans, a clean T shirt, nice sandals, ear-rings. I hear Bella slowly make her way up the ladder to get dressed and race into the bathroom for the quickest of showers. Clean teeth. Brush hair. Rub dry with a towel. Pull on clothes. Deep breath. I run back down stairs, open the front door to let the daylight in. I notice a note on the doorstep.

'I am so happy for you that Bella has come home. I guess it's back to me and Bounce for a few Monday nights, eh? Take care. Terry'.

Ah, sweet man. I stuff the note into my jeans pocket.

I call up 'Hey, are you ready?' as I see her coming backwards down the ladder. I observe her body carefully as it comes into view. She is thin. I watch as she puts her feet on the carpet and swings her body around. Her face is paler than usual. Those dark circles under her eyes are like hollows. But she looks at my face and smiles. 'Yeah, I'm ready.'

The story unfolds slowly over the next two weeks. Her shock, finding out about Peter. The co-incidence of Nick being a sperm donor baby. Nick's plans. Their plans. How it was for her at Nick's place. Her visits home and how much it meant to get the little notes of love and the money each week. The visit to the sperm bank. The premature babies. And then the sudden realisation that they too could be blown up.

I am strangely proud of my Bella. She has, at sixteen, a bravery and commitment and recklessness I have never had in all my adult life. And I am proud that she saw, so clearly, the dangers in what they were planning to do. I kept telling her that. That I am proud of her. She gets that little girl look which used to go with the throw-away accusation, "You're weird, Mum." It takes weeks before I am hit by the criminality of it all. My kid, the terrorist. My kid before the courts. My kid doing time.

I make sure that I do closure with the police at the local station. By now they think I am mad enough for any kid to want to run away from. I make a point of going up there and talking to them about Bella coming home. I tell them she had had enough of running away. They are not surprised. They say it happens all the time. They say kids often come home after the first rainy period or at the first cold snap of winter. I ask them how they close a case. They give me a long explanation which tells me that they do not close it at all. I tell them, the case is closed, now. Bella is home and I want no police records. They tell me they can't destroy her records. They don't say it might help to have the records for when she leaves home next time. If they did I might say I wouldn't want to report it if I couldn't unreport it afterwards. But I don't say anything because I realise that they think I reported it because I thought they would help find her. Well they didn't find her. Waiting for them to find her could have been a very long wait. They tell me that it would be good for Bella to come in and see them, herself.

Over these two weeks, our life returns to some semblance of normality. We start eating real meals, at meal times. We start going to bed at bed-time and getting up in the morning. Bella has gone back to sleeping in her attic, although she spends a lot of time in the spare room, talking to friends on the phone, playing her guitar and, well I'm not sure what else. We see a lot of movies and drive to the beach almost every day, for a long walk.

We start working through the list of things we have to do. I go with Bella to the police and she apologises profusely and admits, yes officer, five weeks is a long time for a kid to spend away without telling her Mum where she is, and, yes officer, she realises that this was a really dumb thing to do, and honestly officer, she certainly will never, ever do it again. And she lies so sweetly when she tells them that they just watched heaps of videos and ate so much pizza she never wants to see one again. Drugs? No, officer, of course not. But yes, problems at school. Yes, she was very unhappy at that school and never felt she belonged. Yes she felt different from the other kids, and some of them did give her a bad time. Tell her mother? No, not really, she didn't think it was all that important. And she listens politely and even contritely while the policeman and the policewoman tell her that children have no idea what they put their parents through when they run away, and that she has done a very cruel and unfair thing to her mother and father and to her other relatives and friends. Yes, yes, says Bella. No, no, says Bella, there is absolutely nothing else she wants to tell them. She can come back any time, if she does? Thank you, thank you all so much. And even worse, I join in with my own thank you, thank you, officer. I fall just short of bowing out of the police station backwards. Thank you.

We have Peter over for a meal, so that we can talk, just the three of us, and we do talk about his shame about his infertility and how that got all out of proportion. Peter apologises for lying to her, and we all talk about the power of secrets in families, and how it can be very destructive. Having cleared up Peter's sins of omission, I smile to myself as Bella plays down the plans that she and Nick were hatching, and plays up the intellectual exercise of seeing how such a thing could be done. She tells Peter that there are very few legitimate ways for teenagers who are pissed off with their families, to take time out from families. She tells Peter that, had she asked, there was no way she would have been allowed to live at Nick's place when his parents were overseas. And we both had to agree with that. But then, Bella admitted that just going ahead and doing it was a bit dumb. That was why she came home and left the tiny flowers. That was her way of telling us she was all right. Yeah. Well Peter and I didn't let her get away completely with that one either.

We have been to see a few local schools, and have settled on one a short train ride away. It is in a more stable middleclass suburb, surrounded by stable middleclass suburbs. There are more houses set in gardens and less high rise flats. There are no corner shops and less mess blowing about in the streets. It is leafier near this school. The streets are a bit wider. The kids come from only seven different language groups instead of the 23 at her old school. The staff we meet are very helpful. They look at the dark circles still under Bella's eyes and ask why she wants to change schools. We say the last one was a bit rough. They nod. Sooner or later we will have to give them a version of the truth. Her school records will be transferred from her old school. There will be notes attached. I make a note to visit the principal at the old school and thank her for all that she and the school have done for Bella. I start rehearsing what I will say to her. How it is a good time for a new start for Bella. Away from Nick.

The weekend before she starts at her new school her friends start dropping in. Some of them are from her old school, but I am relieved to see some others, too. Local kids, who go to private schools. Kids she has gone down to the local pool with. Kids who she has started going to hear music with. It feels so thankfully normal. I feel so thankfully blessed. I don't care how much they eat or drink or how much mess they make, or if they go off for bike rides without their safety helmets or get too buzzy while they drink coffees in the Italian cafes.

I say to the kitchen ceiling, to the water pouring over me from the shower, to the inside of the fridge and to lid of the washing machine, thank you, thank you, thank you for giving me back my girl.

But there is one last twist of the knife. We get a phone call, late one night. It's Meredith, mother of Miranda, Bella's best friend from the old school. I don't know Meredith very well, but she obviously knows about Bella and Nick. She tells me that she is so sorry to have to phone me about this. She understands what we have been through and knows that Bella is starting to recover.

I want to scream at Meredith to cut the crap and just tell me what is so awful. And then I wished to hell that I hadn't heard what she said. When she said, 'Nick has killed himself. Nick hanged himself in the garage of their home. His parents had already got on the plane to come home. Gina, there was no-one else there with the boy. The older brother hasn't been seen by neighbours for weeks.'

All I can manage is an 'Oh no!' and a 'How dreadful' and finally, a 'Thanks, Meredith. Thanks for phoning. Yes. I'll have to do that, right now.'

So I pull myself up the stairs. I heave my suddenly too heavy body up the ladder to the attic, where Bella is lying in bed reading. She sees the look on my face.

'Mum, what is it? What's wrong?'

I wish I knew some easier way of saying this. But I just tell her. I just say it.

'Bella, love. Nick's dead. They think it was suicide.'

Her face crumples. Her body shrinks before my eyes.

'How?'

'He hanged himself in the garage.'

'What's the date?' she asks

I tell her, somewhat puzzled.

'Today was the day we were going to do it', she said. 'I knew he wanted to do it really badly, but, Mum, I didn't know it was that bad. I didn't know he couldn't live without doing it.'

She started sobbing.

'It's my fault.' She started screaming, 'It's my fault. It's my fault.'

'No, baby.' I try to cradle her.

'It's not that I should have done it with him, it's that I should never have said that I would do it with him in the first place.'

I am amazed at her clarity. I try to get my own head clear. I know that I have to say something which makes sense.

'Yes. There is that side to it. But perhaps you had to test yourself out. Perhaps you had to see how close you would go to doing something so dangerous and destructive. And, Bella, there was no way you could have known that Nick could not cope with not doing it. There was no way you could have known that.'

She half buys it.

'Thanks, Mum.'

She reaches out for a tissue and mops up her face. She slides past me.

'Think I'll ring Miranda.'

I am left sitting on her bed. I am no way ready for the ladder. I lie down, like I used to, when Bella was missing. The picture of the volvox is still there, and as I close my eyes I see Nick's family as a very fragile volvox indeed. I wonder what his parents wanted so badly overseas that they left the boys at home for such long periods of time. I wondered what had gone on with Nick's older brother, and what was his story that he was using and selling smack. I wondered about Nick, poor baby, and how a sixteen year old boy could stake his life on carrying out a really dumb idea. I wondered if he knew all along that he would kill himself if he didn't go through with it. I wondered if he somehow hinted at that urgency when he lured Bella into his plan. How do sixteen-year-olds tell if their friends are just a bit mad or really mad? Fuck, how do we tell?

And then I suddenly sat bolt upright, with the realisation that of course I knew. I was just so manically and selfishly grateful to have my Bella home that I pushed down any thoughts or concerns about Nick. I recalled so clearly, like it was being played out then and there in front of my eyes, one night, when Bella had crawled into my bed, and wanted to tell me about running away that last day, from Nick's. And I could hear her voice saying

'And then Mum, he said, 'I'll kill you, Bella', before he locked me in the room.

So why didn't I twig to it? So why didn't I spare a thought for a teenage kid who was so devastated by Bella leaving that he threatened to kill her? Why the fuck didn't I at least visit the kid? Why didn't I alert the school and say that Bella had been at Nick's place all this time and I have good reason to believe that the kid is definitely not all right.

I half heard the phone conversations down stairs. I heard Bella comforting Miranda and long silences while I guess Miranda was comforting Bella and I wondered how on earth they knew how to do that, for each other, at sixteen years of age.

And then I wanted my mum. I wanted my mama to cuddle me and comfort me and tell me, yes, I should have done this and I could have done that, but perhaps it would not have made any difference, and that Nick's need to finish his life at sixteen was laid down a long long time ago.

But she was not there. And I was left with the guilts and the "should haves". And suddenly I felt very old, and very un-nurtured, and wondered how much of me there was left to put out and put out and put out for Bella, knowing that this last and hopefully final straw was not going to break her, but would certainly shake her.

We managed pretty badly, Bella and I, that next few days. The timing between us was bad. I was running empty. I had run out of being the perfect and understanding mother at the same time that she really needed so much more from me. She came up with the solution herself.

'Mum, I'd like to go to Dad's for the weekend. Do you mind? Will you be alright if I go?'

'I'll be OK. Let's phone and I'll drive you over.'

14. BLUE GUM

I drive Bella over to Peter's. Verity's tired and lying down, and Peter is keeping it all together. He has put Sam to bed and read him stories. He has given the three drinks of water and has supervised the following trips to the toilet. He has cleaned up in the kitchen and is now getting clothes ready for the morning. He hugs us both as he lets us in. He is open to being needed. By Bella. Good. I can go.

I go home and lie down on my bed. So, I ask myself. What do I really need, want at the moment? Apart from wanting to be a good mother, and wanting the man in my life to be unmarried. Geoff? Do I want Geoff? Mmmm. Tempting. But no, not tonight. I lie there, and close my eyes, and allow my mind to settle. And it comes to me that tomorrow morning I will wake early and drive to the Blue Mountains and take a long, long walk down into the Blue Gum Forest. Miraculously I fall asleep.

It takes me an hour and a half to drive up to the mountains. I'm feeling tough in my walking boots, khaki shorts, Greenpeace sweatshirt, floppy green hat and backpack. I feel well prepared on this warm early spring day. A picnic lunch for one from an expensive deli, fresh bread from the German bakery and a bottle of water. What else could a woman want? Well, being me, a rolled up rain coat, my swimmers, sunscreen cream, insect repellent and of course my mobile phone which I never use, and which probably doesn't work anymore, just in case. Actually, my pack is not quite as light as I would like.

I park my car just past Mount Wilson, where the track begins. Double check that I have locked it and carefully put the keys in the front pouch of my backpack with my wallet and sunnies. I cream up with sunscreen. Hat on. And start walking.

I had forgotten how wonderful it is to walk by myself. No distractions. Just allowing my eyes to take in the scenery as they will. I smell all the different scents of the plants and leaf litter on the track. I hear the birds and the faint sounds of cascading streams, which I know will get louder and louder as I head away from the road and down into the valley.

Today I feel totally at one with this most ancient of countries. I feel like a dot, moving down a path with the mountains spreading on and on to the north and the south, a giant ridge running the full length of this land and dividing the eastern coastal cities and beachside playgrounds from the empty arid inland. I feel I am a speck on this ridge, travelling east to west, mountain top to valley, each step taking me back through time, away from my job, the city, shopping malls, television, computer screens, down down down with each step, to ancient sacred places.

My mind goes into that wonderful empty space I can never access no matter how hard I try to meditate. No lists forming. No number games. No shoulds. My feet set up a soothing rhythm, my arms swing at my sides, and my body gives into the pull of gravity as it effortlessly follows the empty track down, down, down.

My rhythm is broken as I slow down behind a family. A young couple, Dad with a toddler in a backpack, Mum attentive to a little poppet about five. I manoeuvre a gentle overtake and we exchange "g'day"s. My heart clicks in with a warm rush of love for happy families, quickly followed by an almost exquisite sadness. I try to keep the warm love feeling stay with me, go on stay, just for ten more steps.

I'm walking fast now. Feet heavy on the track. Heavy and fast. Heavier, faster. What is it about me and love? Why do I keep fucking up? Why couldn't I love you in sickness and in health, Peter? Why couldn't I love you through boring conversations and endless lists, Peter? Why aren't I content with the loving you do give me, Geoff? Why do I run empty of good parenting, Bella, at the times she really need me? What's the matter with me? Why can't I do love and keep doing love? Love for the long haul?

I am angry at me but even more I realise I am allowing me to be angry at Bella for what she has just put us through.

Say it. Say her name. Say it out loud. I stop. I step to the edge of the track and face the huge stone escarpment which has suddenly appeared from behind the greenery like a giant backdrop. I take a deep breathe and I scream out. "Bellaaa. Bellaaa. Bellaaa." I tell the emptiness that she is a little shit. I tell it she can't do that again to us.

And then I remember Nick and I say thank you Bella, thank you for coming home. Thank you for being alive.

Alma's voice cuts in.

"Your choice". These are Alma's favourite words. The ones I most hate to hear in our sessions together. Your choice. Your choice. I start walking again. It was not my choice she ran away. Your Choice. It was not my choice to get the scrappy left overs of the wonderful woman my mother once was, and such a miserable lonely childhood. Your Choice. It was not my choice never to see my father. Your Choice. It was not my choice to cut ties with my real family. Your Choice. How can you say all that was my choice? That's so unfair. Your Choice about what you do now. Your Choice for today and tomorrow. Your Choice for the rest of your life. Well thanks a lot!

My feet are now flying down the track. My pack is cutting into my shoulders. I am very thirsty but I will not stop for a drink. I see two very fit old men on the path in front of me. They look like they have been bushwalking mates since forever. Probably poofs. Probably paedophiles. I smile as I brush past them with a dazzlingly friendly "G'day." I can walk faster than they can. Ha. Well, you are about thirty years younger. Who asked you?

What am I doing on this beautiful day, all by myself, crapping on to myself, clomping down a mountain side in the middle of bloody nowhere? My choice. Okay. I calm down a bit, drop my pace a bit, let my heart slow down a bit, match my breaths to my feet, get a rhythm, and notice that the track is levelling off and that the loud noises are not from my head but are the gushing white waters of the river as it flows wide and fast after the recent torrential rains.

The river crossing of half submerged rocks is still there. So is the path with the slippery log. I can do it. With style and confidence which surprise myself, I make the crossing with the white water almost touching my boots. I climb across the boulders. I follow the river upstream, across the rocks, out of hearing shot of the few bushwalkers who have settled down on the scarce flat surfaces, until I reach my favourite spot, thankfully empty. It is a rock shelf, just long enough for me to lie on. There is shade from a huge overhanging Casuarina. The sound of the water is so loud it silences even my head. It feels so good.

I spread out my picnic. I make up a fresh bread roll from the delicacies I have indulged in. Smoked salmon, ricotta cheese, dried tomatoes and a little green salad on the side. Ahh, bliss. Fresh water and a peeled orange. I contemplate a swim, and slide down the rock to feel the water with my outstretched hand. No swim today. Not in that water. I'd freeze. Totally ignoring my sensible self, I take off my boots and socks and place them carefully on the ledge. I balance myself further down the sloping part of the rock, and find a position where I can comfortably balance and put my feet in the rushing water at the same time. Ah. My feet go through a painful adjustment to the cold and then relax.

I let myself go into a blissful switched off state, half awake and half asleep giving in to replays from my childhood. I let in some of the good times. Picnics at this very spot merge with replays from Bella's childhood. Little girls jumping into freezing water, in creeks and rivers, in the waves at Bondi. Games of hide and seek. Birthday parties in the parks.

I am cold. I put my socks and boots back on, gather up my things, and head off back across the rocks. I notice the river spot is now empty. I check my watch and realise that it must have stopped. It's certainly later than 2.15. I suppress the beginnings of panic. Why didn't I think of bringing a torch? Who knows I'm here? No-one, that's who. I check the position of the sun low in the west, and reassure myself that there is at least a couple of hours of sunlight. Two hours down. It will take more than two hours to get back up. Not if you really push it. Okay, girl. Go!

I go. I start up the track. It climbs and climbs and climbs. Steps. More steps. I do not stop. I feel the pain in my thighs and calves. O why haven't I kept fit. Your choice. Damn you. Shut up! I silence any voices. I can't afford any more voices. I tie my lungs to my feet. Breath in for four steps. Out for four steps. I keep my eyes on the tops of my boots. I dare not stop. If my feet stop moving I will stop breathing.

I try not to notice the sun slowly slipping behind the western hills. No, it is not slowly slipping. It damn well rushes the last little bit. But the light lingers. It is still light enough to see the tops of my boots. And the track.

Just as the light fades out I realise that I am going to make it. I recognise the beginning of the track. I indulge myself – guess, go on guess. Okay one hundred and fifty steps to my car. I start to count. I can just make out the outline of the car at step number 113. I stop counting and run for it. Made it.

I sit in the car, in the dark, listening to my breath coming back to normal. The pounding in my ears slows down. Thank you, God of stupid bushwalkers. Thank you. And a pleasure rises in me which has a lot to do with not having to use the mobile.

As I turn on the ignition, I realise how tired I am. Too tired to drive home. An idea forms in my tired brain. I drive further north until I reach the turn-off which will take me to the main Blue Mountains road. As a reward for finding this turn-off I push the button to start Mozart's clarinet concerto on the CD player and it soothes me and keeps me awake as I drive past the familiar road signs. At Mt Victoria I turn east, back towards Sydney down the main highway which passes through all the little towns and villages. I stop at the first Vacancy. Not a motel. No. A small guest house.

The bell on the counter summonses a friendly face, an older woman. Yes, just a single please. Yes a bath would be wonderful.

I have a long luxuriating bath. I duck out briefly for a pizza to take back to my room. I grab an armful of outdated Women's Weeklies from the foyer as I head back. I lie in bed and slowly eat all the slices of pizza and read at least 20 one page stories of people who have experienced all sorts of traumas – breast cancer, a child suiciding, addiction to a prescribed drug, addiction to an illegal drug, a husband who was retrenched after 35 years with the one company, lost at sea in a storm, losing a leg, allergies to everything in the entire world. They all have something in common. They suffered. O Boy how they have suffered! But, in the end, they have all triumphed out of their adversities. Yes. It was tough, but they did it. They survived and more than that, they are now better people and they want to share their tale of survival in the hope that it may help other people who are going through tough times. All in one page each!

And despite my superior attitude, I kept reading these repetitive same-message stories, until the whole pile of those Women's Weeklies had gone from my bed to a mess on the floor and I could reach up and turn off the reading light with a stupid smile on my face and a smugness I could not quite define.

I wake late, and my eyes scan the room, and my brain kicks in and starts wondering where the hell I am. Sore calves remind me. I lie back in the luxury of this super comfortable bed and decide that there is no need for me to rush anywhere today. Bella is not due back till this evening. Today is mine.

I shower, get back into my smelly clothes from yesterday. I try brushing my teeth with soap and a finger but it doesn't work any better than it did when I was a child and forgot my toothbrush at sleepovers. I gather up my few things, and walk down the hall, glimpsing at the dining room and deciding that I do not need to eat from this table with its line-up of sweet juices in pretty jugs, castles of little boxes of cereals or baskets of bread rolls and croissants. I pay my bill and head for the car.

Slowly I turn into the main highway and start the long winding slow descent down the mountains, past the little towns and villages that have been there forever. They have been smartened up in recent years, these little towns, with newly painted shopfronts and cafes with tables and chairs and bright umbrellas on the pavements, but they are still recognisable as the same old places which I had driven past so often as a child. Here was the place with the best milkshakes in the world. Here was the 1920s dance hall converted into a milk bar which sold jars of toffee coated almonds. Here was the second hand store where my mother bought the sparkling chandelier which totally overwhelmed our shabby dining room.

I try to imagine how it must have been for my mother and Teff, all those years ago, when they were tossed out of their home so suddenly, and I wonder why they still chose to come back to the mountains for picnics and bushwalks. I think perhaps they wanted to stay in touch with the place where they had spent so many happy years. I think that perhaps they felt it was still their place, regardless. Their special place of wild beauty, of dramatic sandstone escarpments, of lush valleys and pockets of awesome sclerophyll forests. I feel that closeness to this place. I feel humbled by its ancient natural beauty.

I pick up a sign at the faintly familiar turnoff, a road sign with a big red arrow pointing down the side street, telling the passing traffic in big bold red letters that breakfast is being served all day. I follow the arrow down the narrow tree lined street, and see another red arrow, and another and I keep following the red arrows as they lead me into narrower winding roads and finally to the driveway of a beautiful well established but somewhat neglected garden. I park the car where the signs tell me, and slowly get out, trying to ignore the soreness of my leg muscles which are threatening to make my movements resemble an ancient war veteran.

I sit down at a wooden table, shaded by a large camellia tree. A deep sigh escapes as I take in the overwhelming view and my eyes seek out the most distant mountains. There are wisps of mist floating in the valley below them. Gradually I turn around to get a better look at the big house. A tingling chill starts at the back of my neck and runs down to the base of my spine. I give a shudder as my eyes make out the faded and barely legible ROMA GUEST HOUSE. Hazy toddler memories are stirred. Yes. I have been here before. Yes. Teff took me here before. In his wonderful young mind, all that had to happen was that Uncle Alfredo had to see me, see what a beautiful child I was, see that I had his hair, his eyes, dimples on my knuckles, hands like chubby starfish and little knees that knocked together when I ran, and he would love me and want to see me every day for the rest of his life. Perhaps it is just as well I have no memory of what my father's reaction was, on that day, so long ago.

A woman comes to take my order. She asks if I am alright. I nod. She waits. She suggests a long latte to start with. I nod. She leaves to get the coffee. Come on Gina. Pull yourself together girl. I tell myself I have every right to be here, having breakfast. I notice, for the first time, that the place is almost empty. There is only one couple. Tall and blond and lean, they have to be Scandinavian tourists, reading together from a Lonely Planet guide. They see me looking at them. I smile. They smile. I wonder what the guide book tells them about this place. I wish I had a Lonely Planet so that I could find out whether this place is still in the hands of the Italian family which established the guest house towards the end of the war.

My coffee arrives. My voice is back and I manage a thank you and a big smile. The woman tells me what is on the breakfast menu and I settle for a big meal. Suddenly I am starving.

The Scandinavian couple leave. With their book. I am glad to have the place to myself. When the woman brings my food she asks if I mind is she sits down at the table while I eat my breakfast. She says that it is very quiet at the moment but that she has been on her feet since six this morning and would welcome a rest and a bit of company. But, she says for me to tell her if I want to be left alone.

'No. No. Stay. Of course.' I want to ask her about the guest house fifty years ago, but as she only looks about forty herself, I don't like my chances.

As she sits, I get a better look. I scrutinise her face. How come I was so sure about the Scandinavians and I can't tell if this woman looks Italian?

'So', I say, 'Tell me about the Roma Guest House.'

She tells me that her family started the guest house in the early forties. Some of the men had arrived a long time before, from Italy, to work in the sugar fields in Queensland, and they had saved hard and sent boat tickets back to Italy so that their childhood sweethearts could come out, and so that they could start a family and a family business. She tells me that in its time, the Roma Guest House was the best place in the mountains, and that Italians and other Europeans would drive up from Sydney for their holidays and weekends away. She tells me that it is not the place it used to be. That it isn't even a guest house anymore. She tells me that the old building needs too much money spent on it. She tells me that she is the last of the line. She and her husband do breakfasts all day.

'It's silly really. Breakfast all day. But it's easy. And some tourists like getting up really late and having breakfast in the afternoon. Today', she says, 'is very quiet, for a Sunday. But it might pick up later.'

I sit there, slowly cutting up my poached eggs on toast, adding small amounts of spinach and onions to the fork, getting the fork to my open mouth, chewing, swallowing and sipping the coffee in between. I meet her eyes, and smile encouragingly at her story. Inside, I am such a mess I am amazed that I am going through all these everyday functions.

'I think my family used to stay here,' I lie. 'I think I remember my mother talking about this place. I think I even visited here as a very small child.' Well not such a lie.

I realise that the woman across the table from me is a relative. Cousin? Niece?

'Really?'

'Yes. I remember my mother talking about your family.' My family. 'But of course all that was probably before you were born.'

'Yes. Probably.'

'I remember her talking about the older couple who ran it, and some of the other relatives. Was there an Uncle Alfredo?' That this question has popped out so innocently.

'Uncle Alfredo?' She stops to think. 'Yes, he was a bit of a black sheep. An alcoholic. He died before I was born. They never spoke very much about him.'

Suddenly, I didn't want to speak about him either.

'I wonder if I could have the bill?'

She got up from the table with such an effort. I looked up at her tired face. No, not forty, perhaps thirty at the most.

'I hope I was able to tell you what you wanted to know', she said.

'Yes. Everything. Thank you. What is your name?'

'Rosa.'

'Yes, thank you Rosa.'

15. FUNERAL

The morning of Nick's funeral I awoke to find Bella next to me in the big double bed. She must have crept in during the night while I was fast asleep.

As I came to life slowly shedding the remnants of dreams, I was aware of Bella fast asleep one moment and sitting up wide awake the next.

'Mum. I've never been to a funeral.'

Right. Focus Gina. Focus.

'Are you scared?'

'Well, yes. Like I don't know what to expect, do I?'

'No love, how could you?'

Realising that this last response was pathetic in terms of what Bella obviously needed right now, I tried to go on,

'No one really knows what to expect at a funeral. People behave in all sorts of unexpected ways. Sometimes the very people who you expect to be letting go remain aloof and dry eyed and others, well, others just let go.'

'There'll be a lot of kids from school, too, won't there? There will, you know, and I don't want to see them. And then the teachers will be there and I don't want to see them. And then there'll be Nick's family and I don't want to see them.'

Yes, this was going to be specially hard for Bella. She had not seen most of her classmates from her old school since before she had run away. I wanted to tell her that they would be caught up in their own emotions about Nick but of course I had absolutely no idea how teenagers behaved at funerals. This was way outside my experience. Kids didn't suicide when I went to school. Kids didn't die. At least at the public high school I went to.

'Did Nick have many friends?' I asked

'No' she answered without having to think about it. 'Nick was pretty much a loner. He always had lots to say and he was pretty out there, but he didn't have a girl friend and he didn't seem to have any special friends at all. He just hung out with a big crowd but on the edges.'

'So do you think there will be many coming to the funeral?' I asked

'It's really weird Mum. Last year there was as girl who killed herself in year 12 and although she didn't have too many real friends either, the whole of her class went to the funeral, and her basketball team, too. We heard they were advised to go, like as part of a process, whatever that is.'

'I can see that. It's important to have a ritual. There is something so final about seeing the coffin go into the hole in the ground, or into the fire part of the crematorium. It's a formal goodbye from everyone who loved and knew the person.'

By now Bella was bored with this part of the conversation.

'Dad's coming. Did you know? I asked him on the weekend and he said he'd come too. He said he'd pick us up.'

'Good,' I said.

'God,' I thought.

'OK,' I thought again. 'It's what Bella needs and its good that she can look after herself like that.'

'Bella, it's very brave of you to go to this funeral, you know.'

'I don't feel brave. I'm scared of seeing Nick's parents. I don't know how much they know. I don't even know if they knew I was staying there. I still don't know who knows about that. If they knew, do you think they'd be blaming me? For what happened?'

'No, love. I should think they'd be too busy blaming themselves. How about you having first shower, eh?'

She leaped up at this suggestion.

I lay back, needing to have a few moments with my own thoughts which kept darting back to Nick's parents. My throat tightened as I came as close as I could to imagining what it would be like, being them. Poor, poor things.

My mind darted to how many other funerals there were, this day, all over the world. I reminded myself with over 6 billion people alive at any one time, every breath I took thousands of babies were born and thousands of people died. Babies, starving toddlers, sick children, teenagers like Nick, young adults, middle adults, old adults all dying all the time. And the multiplier of all those families, all sad. I cut off my line of thought. I didn't want to go there.

So I thought about the only other significant death in my life so far, that of my mother Bella. And how comforting was the semicircle of men in their blue and white prayer shawls as they chanted the ancient Hebrew prayers around the grave. How small that funeral was. How few people knew my mother towards the end of her life. How complete it was to see her coffin being lowered into the deep square hole in the earth. How right it felt when Teff shovelled the first sods of clayey soil, thud, on the shiny new wood and then passed the shovel to me, to do likewise and then to Peter who was there in every way, that day.

Peter and I stood together again, close at Nick's funeral. We were way back in the crowd so that we could hardly see the square hole in the ground. But we could see Bella, standing and clutching hands with Melanie, and surrounded by school friends of theirs and Nick's. I kept my eyes on Bella, with a soft gaze so that she didn't feel I was staring at her. I kept sending her messages of love and support. I kept telling her in my mind that she was doing well, and that it was OK if she cried. Keeping a watchful eye on Bella helped my avoidance of Nick's parents and his uncles and aunts, and cousins and grandparents. What an elegant family! Tall and golden genes, there, and a dignity about them, even on a day like this. But I could not bear to look at them. I did not want to share their agony. I could only see the tops of my shoes through blurry eyes as Nick's father's deep cultured voice started saying that no parent ever thinks that one day he will be burying his own child.

I clutched Peter's hand and he squeezed mine. We shared this terrible moment with a closeness we had so rarely experienced during all those years we lived together. In the awful reality of the death of a child and the exquisite relief that the child was not ours. Peter and I were over our anger. We were over our disappointment with each other. There was a tacit understanding that we had been so close, as only young love can be, and that that closeness was now a friendship and a deep sharing of our child.

Meanwhile the very Anglo ceremony was still going on. The very Anglo minister saying prayers and keeping it all together. A very Anglo hymn with voices rising in the bleak cemetery with surprising gusto. A special tribute from the school.

And suddenly it was over. People milled slowly and carefully through the crowd, some reaching out to the family. Some leaving them to themselves. I checked out Bella and she was surrounded by the young people, still firmly hand in hand with Melanie. Peter and I, still firmly hand in hand, joined the stream towards Nick's parents. When our turn finally came, I was lost for words. Peter did well. He said we were Bella's parents and that we were so very sorry about Nick.

I wanted to talk to Nick's parents. I wanted to tell them it was our girl who colluded with Nick and his terrible fantasies. Our girl who was still alive and who seemed to have got off, with no blame from them, no pointing finger, no further involvement from the police. I wanted to thank them for not blaming our girl. I looked at them and guessed that the immensity of their own guilt left no room for Bella, or us, for that matter, for our role as her parents.

But most of all, deep down I craved for that other ceremony and that ancient custom of Jews at funerals walking around and wishing every one else 'Long life'. I felt more pangs of guilt that I was not giving Bella her Jewish heritage. Synagogue was just not on our agenda.

Somehow we got through the rest of that day. Shocked and stunned by reality of the loss of a young life. We splurged on a lunch, just the three of us. We felt guilty eating. We drank a very good bottle of red. Peter and I got into outdoing each other with silly stories about Bella as a young child. Her eyes lit up. We laughed and giggled and felt guilty about that. We made it home and had cups of strong coffee. We all hugged and kissed. And then Peter went back home to his family. And there was just me and Bella, again.

16. ENDINGS

'You've come a long way', Alma says, and my stomach sinks at words I do not want to hear.

'Actually, we have both come a long way', she smiles.

'You know we can't keep going forever, don't you.' And the so familiar words, 'So how are you feeling about that?'

We were just coming to the end of a session, which seemed pretty much like any other session to me. And yes, at one level, I did think we could keep going on forever. Except that this session was full of endings. It was as if the last bits of string from that messed up ball had been unpicked and laid out. We had laboriously followed each one from beginning to end and today we focussed on the last two. Today's strings were not about death, like I thought they would have been, so close after Nick's funeral.

The first was about me and Bella.

I had talked about coming up from the valley that weekend, walking out my anger at Bella for putting through the last few months of hell, and finding that, despite a slight error of timing, I was quite capable of being myself, by myself, for myself. That, no matter what else, I still had me.

'Yes?'

'Yes, that walk down into the valley. Coming back up it felt like I was getting lighter and lighter. It was like shedding a load that I had been carrying and didn't need to carry any longer.'

'What was that load?'

'It was feeling a failure at being Bella's mother. Like it has been the most important thing I will ever do, being her mother, and so often I felt I was second rate. Then, her going like that was the final straw. I really knew I was a failure then. No-one else's kids ran away. I was beside myself with worry over her, but I was also so ashamed. Like, what is her running away really saying about me as her parent? But since she's been back, I've come to understand that this was her thing. Something she had to do, some challenge she had to set herself, even though it was so big for a kid her age. Sometimes, I am in awe of her courage. Yes, she's impulsive and if you like irresponsible but she's no woos, my Bella. She's strong. And perhaps I can give myself some credit for some of that.'

'And I'm feeling better about pulling back a bit, not being in her face. She's not a little kid any more, and although I know I'll always be her mother, the mothering changes, doesn't it? And I am beginning to get a handle that I can change my sort of mothering. Does that make any sense?'

'Yes, it makes good sense.'

'Well, I feel OK about moving off that one.'

'Good.'

'And', and I said to Alma, 'there is more to it, isn't there? Moving off to the next stage gives me more room for me looking after me better, doesn't it?'

'There always has been room for that.'

'Yes, but when there is just the two of us, just me and her, it is so much more intense, somehow. Just one kid and just one parent. There's no distractions. It's all centre stage. But I don't want it centre stage any more. I really want to get my life back. More than that, I am no longer so scared about getting my life back.'

'Yes. What do you think was so scary about that.'

And for the first time, I could look at that with absolutely dry eyes. No prickle in throat.

'Fear of failure.' I said, as if it were the most matter of fact thing in the world. I tried it again. 'Fear of failure.'

That was the second last bit of string.

The very last one finished at the younger Rosa. The door softly closed on all those hours of my life, hungry for the family I never even had. I can do my own dancing now and make my own music.

Instead I say,

'I have a family. Bella is my family. Teff is my family. That's all I have and that's OK. This hanging out for what I never had is finished. It's run its course.'

'And so has this, Gina. It's run it's course.'

Alma looked strangely formal as she held out her hand.

I crossed the boundary of good client behaviour and gave her a big hug. She felt surprisingly tiny and fragile in my big arms, as I whispered 'Thank you, thank you.'

She pulled back and smiled.

'You know you can always phone me, don't you. And you'll know if you need to come to see me. But I have a strong feeling,' she said, 'that you will all be alright now. Not dead easy, mind. But alright. Better than alright,' she added.

And it was over. Another ending for another string.

That night I told Bella.

'So you're OK now, eh?'

'Well, Alma seems to think so. What do you think?'

'Yeah' she said somewhat grudgingly. 'But it's not as if you're going to live happily ever after, is it?'

'No?'

'I mean, like you and Geoff. It's messy.'

I didn't need this. I had had enough for one day. That final session had been big for me and all I wanted was for the clock to move on until it was OK to go to bed.

'How do you mean, messy?'

'Well, it's not what you want and it's not what he wants, so it's messy.'

'Go on,' I said, feeling that Alma had reincarnated in front of me.

'Well, honestly Gina.' She had taken to calling me Gina over the past few weeks and I rather liked it.

She went on, 'You think the problem is that he's the one who's tied down and if he just left his wife then the problem would be solved. But just look at all the tying down you do to yourself.'

Suddenly my elation at finishing over years of counselling therapy was totally deflated by my teenage daughter's analysis of my love life. I put down the urge to scream at her about what exactly had tied me down for the past 16 years. Would she like to look in the mirror?

'Like what, Bella. You've got to explain it to me.'

'Well, it's like you think you are powerless in all this and that it's all Geoff's fault because he won't move out of home, and that since you can't do anything about it, you can just hang about and be the victim. Perhaps it's too hard for you to have a proper relationship with Geoff and so it suits you not to make any decisions or commitments.'

'Mmm.'

'Gina, don't you see what you are doing? You tie yourself down to me and here, just as much as he ties himself down to her and there. You have turned single motherhood into a big tying down scene. You tie me down and you tie yourself down. On the surface we live a pretty normal life. But you feel that if I am home, then you have to be home to do what I can never work out because I don't need you to do anything and you don't do much anyway.'

She paused for breath.

'Gina. I have been able to cook food ever since I could drag a chair over to the microwave. I can throw my clothes in the washing machine and take them out, and hang them and fold them and put them away. I know, sometimes I leave the last bit out. Gina, I'm nearly seventeen. Soon I'll be old enough to leave home. I don't mean run away. I mean, really leave home and move into a shared house. So what is all the tying down about? Why do you have to watch over me? Why aren't you out there having more of a life?'

I caught myself looking at the face of the defiant three year old Bella, stamping her foot and saying 'I won't so!' meaning she wouldn't wear dresses, or eat anything green, or relinquish her smelly comfort rag to the washing machine or kiss Peter's father. And now she was just being more grown up, saying she won't play into my need to protect her, to keep her as a child, to show that I could be a better mother.

I fell back on the old trick of deflection.

'It's hard,' I said, 'isn't it, being an only child.'

But she wasn't going to let me dump it back to her.

'I think it's hard for you, Gina, to be a single mother, especially to an only child. Like you've got all your eggs in one basket. Like you can't afford to stuff up.'

I nodded.

'I know what you're saying. It's taken half a day's pay every week for a chunk of my life, but, you know, I've finally worked that one out for myself.'

'Gina, I know that I've just stuffed up, big time. It's been great that you were here to help me – with the Tuesday notes and the money and I know that must have been so terrible for you, to know and not to know that I was OK. And then fixing me up when I came home such a mess, and now, with Nick and everything. But you can't fix up all my messes. Only I can do that. And you can't stop me getting into the next mess either.'

'Yes. Thank you for telling me all that.'

I tried to keep the sarcasm out of my voice. I succeeded in keeping my hands from grabbing her skinny shoulders and I managed not to give them a good shake while I shouted that she would never, never, know how hard it has been for me.

Instead, I did new good mother,

'Yes. But it's going to be different from now on.'

I looked at her and wondered how come she knew so much. It was like she was reading my thoughts.

'You've taught me heaps, Mum. I am only dealing back lots of stuff I've learnt from you.'

'Yeah. Well, thanks for that.'

And we gave each other a big hug.

I needed to be by myself. I needed to make some sense of my last session with Alma, and my last session with Bella. I needed to consolidate it all, and work out how it was going to be different, from now.

'I'm just going out for a walk', I called out. I did not say that there was some left over dinner from last night in the fridge, or plenty of salad vegies or that it was dark soon and didn't she want to take her clothes in before they got damp.

But I didn't do any of the thinking I set for myself either. I didn't do any of that. I just walked. A long walk. Up to the shops and along the main street, feeling just one of the crowd. Coming home felt good. A note from Bella to say she and Miranda were taking in a movie.

But there was still a restlessness. A need to walk around the little house, through the living room to the kitchen to the laundry and out to the back yard and back again, up the stairs to the spare room, up the ladder and into Bella's room and I noticed that something was different, something had been removed. I sat on her bed and looked around, and noticed the faded square where the picture of the volvox had been hanging. I wondered why Bella had taken it down, and where it had gone. I climbed back down the ladder, walked through the spare room and into my own bedroom. I flopped on the bed and stared at the peacocks in the corners of the pressed metal ceiling.

There was a bubble rising from deep down in my brain. And if I took notice of it, it would drop back down. I had to let it rise to the surface totally unattended. When it stopped rising and allowed me to look I could see that it wasn't a bubble at all. It was the volvox. It had burst, and all the little cells were on their own.

The phone rang,

'Geoff?'

'I've moved out', he said. 'I've rented a studio apartment, just down the road from you. It's unit 4 in number 46. I've just cooked us dinner. Please come over.' And then his voice became irresistibly deep. 'It could be a late night.'

I wrote a note and put it on the fridge under the duck magnet.

'Could be out all night. See you in the morning. God bless.'

ACKNOWLEDGEMENTS

Thank you to my partner Hans, my family and friends who give me the positive love that has very little to do with writing but everything to do with keeping me enthralled with life. Thank you Evan Shapiro for creating Cilento Publishing, inviting me into the enterprise and doing all the boring hack work and thank you, my sister Leone and her red pen.

AUTHOR BIOGRAPHY

Sandra Heilpern cares deeply about environmental and social justice issues. She does not consider herself a writer and only does so when she can no longer deny that 'something' just has to get out.

For more titles from Cilento Publishing go to

www.cilentopublishing.com